D1153333

Please return / renew by date shown
You can renew it at:

CRY FOR KIT

CRY FOR KIT

Veronica Heley

CHIVERS

British Library Cataloguing in Publication Data available

This Large Print edition published by AudioGO Ltd, Bath, 2013.
Published by arrangement with the Author.

U.K. Hardcover   ISBN   978 1 4713 1999 0
U.K. Softcover   ISBN   978 1 4713 2000 2

Copyright © Veronica Heley 1976

Printed and bound in Great Britain by
MPG Books Group Limited

ONE

'Kit! Kit Jeffries!' The voice hissed at me from the dark alley.

I was intrigued, because nobody had called me Kit Jeffries for eighteen years and one month, not since I married Pat Neely in New York in spite of everything his friends had had to say against the marriage. They'd been proved wrong, because Pat and I had had a good time in our marriage, and I include the years in which he was dying and we had both known it.

'Who is it?' I shaded my eyes against the glare of the lamp under which I stood, and peered into the unlit alley. I was standing in the new shopping precinct—new since my day, that is—having just come through the alley from the Market Square beyond. It looked as if someone had followed me. I could make out that there was a dark figure standing just beyond the lamplight, but I couldn't identify him—or was it her? The voice was a hoarse whisper, quite unrecognisable. The big city hummed with life in the still, summer night.

'Come here!' Whoever it was, he or she seemed to be dressed in black. I'm not a big woman, even in high heels, and I could see that the person who had called to me was taller than I was.

1

'Is it Jack?' I asked, stepping nearer. There were a few people crossing the shopping precinct, but no-one was within fifteen yards of me. I had no intimation of danger as I walked out of the light into the alley, for this was my homeland, in which I had lived until I was seventeen. This was not New York, where I wouldn't have dreamed of going for an unaccompanied stroll after dinner for fear of being mugged.

I didn't even see my assailant. Something thick and dark descended over my head and shoulders and I was sent reeling into the ancient brick wall of the alley. Even as I fell, I remembered the actions Pat had drilled into me to avoid the worst effects of a mugging. Roll away from them as you fall. Act dead. Let them take what money or jewellery they want. Don't move until they've gone.

I rolled away from my attacker, cursing myself for having brought my purse with all my traveller's cheques and passport in it. I was also wearing a very beautiful and costly pair of emerald earrings, Pat's last gift to me.

I could feel the thud as something metallic struck the pavement beside my head. I acted dead. I couldn't see a thing with that heavy material over my head. I remembered to let my fingers relax and spill my purse on to the stone pavement, and I listened.

Heavy breathing. Fingers at my wrist. Oh, please don't take my engagement ring! Fingers

2

withdrawn, followed by a distant tinkle. My charm bracelet? Oh, no!

Why didn't someone come?

Something caught me between the ribs, hard. I'd been kicked. I began to wonder if it wouldn't be worth while shrieking for help, when the voice came through again.

'You'll leave tomorrow if you know what's good for you!'

I began to get angry. I haven't got red hair for nothing, and even at the ripe age of thirty-six, I was fit enough to welcome a fight. But even as I fumbled with the material over my head, someone entered the alley from the direction of the shops, and I heard my attacker run off, back towards Market Square.

'You all right?' the newcomer asked. He was a young man with long hair, wearing jeans and a brilliant T-shirt. He helped me to my feet. I looked down the alley, but my assailant had disappeared.

'Quite all right, thank you. A bruise or two. Did you get a good look at the mugger?'

'Sorry. By the time I realised something was wrong, he'd gone. I'm afraid my boots made a row as I reached the alley, and that's what frightened him off.'

It was true that the alley resounded to the slightest sound. I groped about on the pavement for my purse, which was open. I checked that I still had my engagement ring. I did.

The young man helped me back into the lights of the shopping precinct, which made me feel twice my age. Luckily the white silk of my dress was only slightly marked, and my hair looks better ruffled than brushed into a smooth style. His lips pursed in a silent whistle, and I knew he was going to take some shaking off.

'Thanks, I'm all right now,' I said, checking the contents of my purse. Everything was there, including my passport and travellers' cheques. All I had lost was my charm bracelet, which had sentimental value but wouldn't be worth auctioning at Sotheby's.

'You're a stranger here? American?' He put his hand back under my elbow and pressed it.

'I've lived in America for a long time, but I was born here. Thank you, you've been a great help. I don't know what I'd have done if you hadn't come along. Nothing's missing except a piece of costume jewellery. If you could see me through the alley back into the Square? I'm staying at the White Lion Hotel.'

He wasn't eager to see the last of me. 'The police? I could ring them for you. I'm supposed to be meeting my mate, but . . .'

'Oh, no, thank you. That's not necessary.' Walking back through the alley, his feet caught in something lying on the pavement. It was a woman's black coat, made of poor-quality cloth. I remembered it had smelt of sweat and face powder.

The lad frowned. 'Was this used on you? Lady, you should go to the police. If someone brought this to the alley to use on you, then that means the robbery was premeditated, and . . .'

'Nonsense,' I said. 'I wore it myself. It's not mine, but a friend's. I went out for a stroll to see if the city centre still looked the same, and borrowed it.' I took the coat off his arm and gave him my hand to shake. 'Thanks a million. You were terrific.'

He swallowed it, as I knew he would. He didn't want to let go of my hand, but we were within sight of the hotel, and people were passing in and out of the ballroom beside it. He knew I had only to raise my voice to summon help. He went away reluctantly, looking back to see if I might change my mind.

My knees warned me to find a seat, and be quick about it.

Not Edward! I thought. Please don't let it be Edward!

Yet it had to be someone I'd known in the past, someone who had cause to fear my return and who knew about the bracelet. Who else but Edward?

I needed a drink. I was no candidate for Alcoholics Anonymous, but I'd always enjoyed a drink. Pat had taught me to drink beer, but back in England again I'd taken to brandy and dry ginger. Sustained by a vision of a double measure of brandy, I tottered into the hotel.

5

'Hello! Turned up again, has it?' said the receptionist. He took the black coat off me and hung it on a rack in the lobby. 'Someone left it here during the week, and we've been waiting for them to collect it.'

So anyone passing through the lobby might have picked the coat up in passing. Bang went my only clue as to my assailant's identity, but perhaps I could unearth another.

'You've been busy tonight. Has there been much coming and going while I've been out for my stroll?'

'All the time. Always the same when we've a function on in the ballroom.'

He turned away to give his attention to some new arrivals—people I didn't know— and I stiffened my legs and ordered them to take me to the cloakroom. Afterwards, I tried to find a seat in the bar, but it was so crowded that I ordered a drink brought to me in the lounge instead.

If only it were not Edward!

It had to be someone I knew, because they had called me by my maiden name. It had to be someone from the past, who didn't know that I was registered at the hotel as Mrs Patrick Neely. It had to be someone who had seen me that night.

I had only arrived back in the U.K. two days ago, had spent one day shopping in London, and returned by train to my birthplace at two o'clock that afternoon. I had not seen

6

anyone I knew on the train, and I had taken a taxi from the station through the sprawl of the ancient city, through the towering blocks which had replaced the slums, and out to the pleasant suburb in which my sister lived. It was a big city and it had grown since my day. Once it had been a market town, but now it was given over to industry.

I had spent the afternoon with my sister and her husband, Tom, and seen no one else I knew. Both Mary and Tom wanted me to disappear again, but I couldn't see either of them stalking me down dark alleys, and neither would have been interested in my charm bracelet.

From my sister's house I had taken another taxi to the hotel. I had registered, unpacked, dined and settled myself in the hotel bar for the evening. I wanted to be quiet. I needed to think over the problem of Mary and Tom, and plan my next move. I had been unhappy, and missing Pat.

Up till a year ago I had thought to live out the rest of my life in the States, but when Pat could no longer run his various business enterprises efficiently, he began to worry about my future. He had done well since I had married him, and he was worth a lot of money. He sold all his companies and invested the money for me. He had long discussions with me about his past, the things he had done, and the things he had left undone. He was afraid

7

I would be lost without him, because I am the kind of woman who needs a man to fuss over. He said he was worried I might be wooed after his death by men who wanted me for my money, rather than for my looks or kind heart. He was obsessed with the idea that I ought to return to England and claim my son.

'No mourning,' he said. 'You must marry again, but wisely. There is still time for you to have another child, to make up for our failure . . .'

'No failure,' I'd said. 'You know I didn't care.'

'You cared, but you were loyal, and we did well enough. However, there is your son to consider. He has the right to meet you and the right to know his father's name. He'll be eighteen soon.'

'You know I promised my sister that I'd never try to see him. I even signed a paper to that effect on the day I handed him over to her.'

'Things are different now. You were only seventeen then, the boy's father couldn't marry you, your parents were unsympathetic, your sister barren, and you had no money or place to live. All these years you've sent money for his keep and in return received a progress report and a snapshot from your sister once every six months. That's not much. It was only natural for your sister to fear you would try to take him from her when he was a child, but

8

at eighteen he should be about ready to leave home himself, or at least be capable of making his own decisions. When he's old enough to vote, he's old enough to know the truth. Think what it must have been like for him to grow up without knowing whose son he is . . .'

'Do you think I haven't worried about it? But if Edward won't acknowledge the boy, what good would it do to tell Johnny who his father is?'

'He has a right to know. I see now that I've been very selfish, Kit. I ought to have helped you in this. I didn't do so because I wanted you all to myself. I ignored your grief . . .'

'Not grief, darling. I've longed for him sometimes, it's true, but . . .'

'Grief, Kit. Do you think I haven't noticed how the sight of children affects you? And a certain type of man?'

He meant men of Edward's type; big, handsome, fair-haired and intelligent. Luckily I hadn't met many such in the years I'd been married to Pat.

'I've only looked at two other men in all these years, and I confined myself to looking. You know I'd never have left you.'

'I had an unfair advantage, didn't I? You wouldn't leave a dying man.' Pain took over his body at that point, and I made him stop talking. But later he whispered, 'Loving and giving, that's you. I'm a lucky man. I'd have gone under years ago if it hadn't been for you.

And what do I have to leave you? Only money. I ought to have taken you back to Europe last summer while I could still walk. I could have made it easy for you. I was jealous of your son, and of his father. I thought they might take you away from me.'

'Idiot! I think of Johnny often, but I know he is loved and happy. As for Edward, he is still married and he has his legitimate son to look after. What could he have to say to me now, or I to him?'

'I want you to promise me you'll go back as soon as my body is disposed of. Go back to where you belong. Your sister . . . the boy . . . you will have money . . . they may need it . . .'

He'd made it all sound so reasonable that, to ease his mind, I'd promised. Neither Mary nor Tom thought it reasonable, though. I wrote from America to ask if I might meet Johnny while on a forthcoming visit to Europe. They replied forbidding it, and reminding me of my promise never to try to see my son again. In spite of that I telephoned Mary from London to warn her I was coming. She arranged for the boy to be out of the house and denied knowledge of his whereabouts. I didn't blame her. She said she'd asked the boy if he wished to meet me, and he had replied that he didn't see the point of it. And would I please go away and leave them in peace.

So I had taken a taxi to the hotel, changed and dined. Afterwards I had moved to the

10

bar and, sitting on a high stool facing the mirror behind the shelves of spirits, I found I had taken a ringside seat at a review of my past life. The bar was in a recess to one side of the hotel lobby, and opposite was a short corridor leading to the hotel ballroom and the cloakrooms. There was another door into the square at the far end of the corridor, so that guests who were attending a function in the ballroom need not pass through the hotel proper. I never did find out what function was being held in the ballroom that night . . . Rotary Club . . . Conservative Club . . .? But most of my contemporaries seemed to be attending it, and as I sat there I could see them arrive either through the lobby behind me, or through the door at the end of the corridor.

It was enthralling.

I saw Paul and Joan first, and that seemed only right and natural, for it was Paul who had introduced me to his friends, and to Edward, so many years ago. Paul was the son of a rich man and already established as a director in his father's firm, and yet with all his wealth he had such compassion and such a clear head that he was the natural leader of the group.

I had been selling stockings, fresh from school, in the city's biggest store when he met me. I was a virgin, and Paul made no attempt to alter that state of affairs. It was hard now to remember exactly how many boys I had gone out with that year. There had been maybe eight or nine boys in the group, each with their satellite girls, but I suppose I had been out with some four or five of them. Although I did not belong in their set by birth, I was acceptable because I was the prettiest girl they knew and also because I was a good listener. My parents were pleased, because they thought going out with members of the group would increase my chances of making a good marriage. My sister Mary was some fourteen years older and had already been married ten years by that time; I hardly knew her.

It was Paul who had given me the bracelet and a gold horseshoe charm to hang upon it. He called it The Queen's Tribute, and it became a point of honour for any boy who gained my favour to present me with another charm. They were as nice a crowd of youngsters as you'd wish to meet anywhere, and even though one of them eventually forced me to surrender my virginity, I bore him no grudge for what was, at bottom, a misunderstanding on his part. I had three offers of marriage in six months, but declined them all, because I was in love with Edward.

Edward Straker. He was the elder son of Councillor Straker, who owned a printing works. Mrs Straker had died young and the two boys, Edward and Jack, had been brought up in a dark, chilly house by a father who worshipped respectability and punctuality. Jack had escaped into childish illnesses and laughter; he had a ready tongue and made friends easily. For Edward there was no such escape. His brain was quicker than his tongue, he was sober and reliable. And reserved for Amy Coulster before I met him.

I fell in love with him the moment I saw him, and raged at myself for my stupidity. Why did I have to choose the only man in the group who was unobtainable? I was pretty, and lively, and a good dancer, so why did I have to handicap myself when so many nice boys wanted me to concentrate on them? I knew I couldn't compete with Amy, who was poised, and dressed well, and knew how to be witty and flatter a man. She was no pin-up, but she had all the wealth of Coulsters' Mills behind her, and it was rumoured that Edward was to be made a director of the giant works on the day of his marriage. The Coulster blood had run thin in Amy's generation, and they welcomed the brilliant young accountant into their ranks for his brains, as well as his engagement to the Chairman's only daughter.

So I went out with other boys and tried not to watch Edward when we were at parties together. Soon I discovered that he was watching me, too. We did not speak to each other; well, perhaps half a dozen sentences in as many months. 'Pass the salt, will you?' 'Going in Fred's car?' That sort of thing. I could not bear to see him, and yet I could not keep away from him.

I went out with Jack not only because I liked him enormously, but also because he was the nearest thing I could get to Edward. There was bad blood between the brothers in those days. Jack was as frank as Edward was reserved and it was not hard to see how they had come to dislike one another. Jack had been his mother's favourite—perhaps because he was so often ill and needed her more than his healthy elder brother—and Edward had felt himself rejected by her. Edward, on the other hand, had the looks and stamina which Jack lacked, and for these things his younger brother envied him. To make matters worse, Edward was his father's favourite, and after Mrs Straker's death Edward had been cast as the 'goody' and Jack as the 'baddy' in every family dispute.

Jack used to bait Edward, which made me feel sick. I tried to stop Jack, explaining that Edward was very thin-skinned and felt it when his brother made fun of him. After all, I said, Edward could never retaliate physically because Jack was so much smaller than he. It did no good. I learned to leave the room when Jack started on his brother. Apart from that, Jack and I had a marvellous time that summer; dancing, laughing, going on car rallies, and making love in the back of his old banger. We even talked of marriage.

When Jack went away to university and the date of Edward's marriage drew near, I tried to drop out of the group, because I was only hurting myself by continuing to see him. Then Paul rang me one night to ask me to a party at his house. His parents were to be away and so, he told me, was Amy. She had gone up to London to choose her wedding dress. Perhaps I imagined it, but I thought at the time that Paul was deliberately throwing me in Edward's way. I went, by myself.

Edward was there. We looked at each other and as usual did nothing about it. I had plenty of offers to dance. Someone—I think it was Tinker—spilt his drink down my dress. I couldn't afford to have it spoiled, so I rushed upstairs to see if I could sponge out the stain. The bathroom was engaged. I thought one of the bedrooms might have a washbasin in it, and tried doors until I found one which had.

Edward followed me in, and closed the door.

As usual, we stared at each other. It was the first time we'd been alone.

'I'm sorry about your dress,' he said. 'Will you let me pay to have it cleaned?'

'It will be all right, I think.' I went on rubbing at the stain, thinking how marvellous it was that he should have noticed I was in trouble and tried to do something about it. I was very conscious of him.

He waited until I had finished, but didn't move from the door to let me out. He held out his hand, with a gold charm on his palm. A gold heart.

He cleared his throat. 'Is that right?' His voice went high and low on him.

'I don't take presents for . . . I'm not that kind of girl.'

'I d-didn't mean . . . I know that you're . . . Kit, please!'

He was stammering, as pale as I was red. I couldn't refuse him because he needed me so badly. He wasn't particularly good in bed, but he was everything I'd ever wanted in a man, and I didn't care that he wasn't as practised as Tinker, or as his brother Jack. I thought of all the caresses I could teach him, and I felt dizzy with joy. It was quick and violent; we had been building up to it all that year, and we had to get it out of our systems. From the way he kissed me and held me, I thought he loved me as much as I loved him. Foolishly I laid myself open to rebuff.

'You won't marry Amy now?'

'I must.'

'But I love you!'

He said it again. 'I must.' He put the gold heart on the coverlet and went to the door. I called his name. He looked back.

I screamed, 'You should take lessons from your younger brother!'

My wicked tongue! If I'd thought for a month, I could not have devised a more damaging thing to say. He faltered. He tried to open the door the wrong way, then mastered

16

the trick of it and left. By the time I rejoined the party he had gone, and after that I took care not to go anywhere he might be.

When I discovered I was pregnant I telephoned his home. I was told he was away on his honeymoon. I spoke to his father and left a message asking Edward to call me on his return. He failed to do so.

I wrote. He replied sending me five hundred pounds in fivers and asking me not to bother him again. He wrote that I probably had plenty of other men in tow who could be blackmailed into supporting me and my illegitimate child when the five hundred pounds ran out.

At first I simply stared at the letter. I could not believe that Edward would act like that. Then I wanted to kill him. Then I wanted to kill myself.

I told my family. They were furious. They demanded to know who the father was. I said I didn't know. They said I must leave home, that they would never be able to hold up their heads again, that I was a wicked girl and they wished I'd never been born.

So did I.

The doctor said I was a Natural Mother and would have no trouble in breeding. He was right. If only I'd been allowed to keep the child, I think I'd have adjusted to the shock in time, but in those days you were expected to keep out of sight until after the birth, hand the baby over to be adopted, and move away to make a fresh start. I couldn't bear the thought of giving my child away. I cried and cried. I lost my job. I had crazy dreams in which I forced my way into Edward and Amy's beautiful new house and committed suicide on their carpet, but I still refused to divulge his name to anyone. If Edward felt that way about me, then I'd have nothing more to do with him.

Then Con Birtwhistle, who was Jack's best friend and an absolute poppet, met me in the street one day and carried me off for a pot of tea. He insisted on hearing the whole story and for the first time I was glad to tell it. Like Paul, Con cared about people. He was very distressed by my tale, and if I hadn't shown him Edward's letter, I don't think I'd have been able to convince him that I was telling the truth. He wanted to go to see Edward straight away, but I stopped him. What was the use? Anyway, the fault was half mine.

Con kept me sane through my last month of pregnancy, calling to see me most evenings for a chat. Although we were never lovers, he gave me the last of the charms I collected in England—a crown for the Queen of Hearts. He said that I had a great gift for loving which I must learn to use wisely.

It was Con who suggested that my sister Mary might take the child when it was born. She was years older than I, a plain girl with whom I had never got on. Mary and Tom had long ceased to hope for a child of their own, and they agreed at once, provided that I left the country within a month of the child's birth, and promised not to see him again. They didn't trust me not to cause trouble if I stayed. I'm sure they were right.

What ought I to have done? I wonder about it even now. Everyone said I was doing the right thing by going. I did as they wished. I handed over my baby and half the money Edward had sent me, and stepped on a plane to New York.

I suppose things had worked out well enough. Mary and Tom had had a child to care for, Johnny had had a loving home, Edward had been left in peace to cherish Amy and their son Piers, and I had a seat on the plane next to a middle-aged, red-headed construction engineer named Pat Neely. Pat had just been through the divorce courts and was bitter about it; he was returning to America from a business trip to London, in order to face exploratory surgery for cancer. He was drinking heavily. By the time we got to New York he had stopped drinking and we had heard each other's life stories. There and then Pat had taken my hands and said he wasn't going to let me go.

'Maybe it will only be for a few months,' he'd said. 'But I know when I'm on to a good thing, and I'm not letting go of you without a fight.'

'Nor are you letting go of life without a

fight, I hope!'

'I'll pay you a thousand dollars for every month you stay with me!'

'Nonsense,' said I. 'I'll come for my keep and a monthly cheque to send Mary for the baby.'

So that was how Pat and I had come to meet and marry, and live happily until the cancer finally took over and Pat died, returning me to base.

Returning me to Edward, who had just tried to kill me.

There couldn't be any doubt about it, could there?

*   *   *

I went over the sequence of events for that evening in my mind, just to make sure.

First I had seen Paul and Joan. Paul Barnes, now M.P. for South Ward. He'd put on weight since I'd last seen him, but he looked well. He hadn't seen me, and neither had Joan. She was wearing a severely cut brocade evening dress and a good mink stole; a far cry from the tousled, informal look she'd affected in the old days. I had always liked Joan. She had been the only one of the girls in the group who had been friendly with me, especially after I'd resigned Paul to her care. I grinned, thinking of the way Joan and I had been accustomed to stir things up. Joan knew all about my friendship with Paul, so even if I did still wear his bracelet and charm, why should he worry? I could rule out the notion that Paul might have attacked me.

Besides, neither Paul nor Joan had seen me.

Jack had, though. He came in through the hotel lobby, with a tall, dark woman who was a stranger to me. Jack was still ash-blond, bony, and middling-sized. And talkative.

He'd rushed over and hugged me, half dragging me off my stool.

'Kit! Great heavens, is it really you? You're twice as lovely, and that's saying something! I can't believe it!'

His companion looked annoyed. 'Jack!' she said, trying not to sound angry. He introduced us; Marge Lawrence, a clever interior designer who often worked with him. Marge, it was plain, wanted to do more than work with him; she wanted him for keeps. It was equally plain to me that Jack wasn't interested in her that way. He held my hands and radiated pleasure, talking nineteen to the dozen, just like old times. For the first time since my return, I felt as if Pat's advice had been sound.

'Dear Jack!' I said, when I could get a word in, 'Con wrote to tell me about your wife's death. I grieve for you.' His wife had had one miscarriage after another until the doctor put her on the pill. It disagreed with her, she had had a thrombosis and dropped dead one morning while out shopping. Jack had found it

21

very hard to carry on after that.

His eyes went wide and blank for a second. Then he grinned.

'Kit, I'm, glad you're back. We've missed you.'

'For eighteen years?' I laughed, but I felt he was sincere. Dear Jack, so sweet and so tough under that misleading air of fragility! Jack had had rheumatic fever and every other ailment you could think of in childhood, and yet had survived to marry a fellow student and become a successful architect. I hoped it was true that he and Edward were now on better terms.

He pressed the rings on my left hand. 'Why did you run away as soon as my back was turned? Going off to America without a word to your friends . . .'

'Who told you?'

'Con, of course. I'm no good at letter-writing, never was. I told him to tell you how sorry I was to hear about your husband. Have you enough money for the time being? Do you want a job, because if so, I might be able to . . .'

'I'm fine for the moment. Thanks, Jack, but I may only be here for a few days . . .'

'Nonsense!'

Marge put her hand on his arm, to remind him that he was her escort for the evening. With well-concealed annoyance he took her off to the ballroom, promising to phone me in the morning. No, Marge hadn't liked me one little bit, but I was used to being disliked by other women. I'd always been a honeypot and if men preferred my company to that of their wives, I wasn't going to discourage them; in my experience men were far more interesting to talk to than women. And I don't mean to flirt with, either. I wouldn't have played Pat false for anything.

It hadn't been Jack who had attacked me. He couldn't have cared less who saw us embrace in the hotel bar and it would never have occurred to him to rob me of my charm bracelet for the sake of a tiny gold crown.

Yet surely the only reason why anyone would take the bracelet was because they thought it might incriminate them. There were twenty-four charms on it, eighteen of them given to me by Pat as anniversary presents, and six given to me by the men who had squired me around in the year before I left.

Paul had started my collection, Fred, Tinker and Jack had added to it, Edward had given me the heart and Con the crown. Fred . . . Tinker . . . Jack . . . Edward . . . their faces whirled round and round in my mind, mixing with the faces of other men and women from my past who had been reflected in the mirror that evening. A kaleidoscope of figures, fat, thin, tall, short . . . kind and unkind . . . ugly and handsome . . . Edward!

Still handsome. At thirty-six, knowing all I did know about him, I ought to have been

23

able to meet his eyes in a mirror and stand my ground. Edward and Amy had arrived in a clump of people through the door at the end of the corridor. I recognised at least one other member of the party, but couldn't for the moment put a name to his face. I saw Amy first. She was wearing a superb bronze silk dress, but she looked discontented, her face more deeply lined than it ought to be at her age. She was frowning around, checking up on the members of her party, fidgeting with a fine diamond bracelet on her bare arm.

Edward, head and shoulders over her, looked what he was; a successful business man who had long driven any spontaneity of feeling underground. His hair was paler in colour than it used to be, almost approximating to Jack's ash-blond, but his jaw-line was as hard as ever, his eye as blue, and his shoulders even broader than I had remembered. He turned at his wife's request to look for the missing member of their party, and saw me in the mirror.

For a few seconds he relaxed his usual control over his facial muscles. I read puzzlement in his eye, succeeded briefly by a flash of triumph or joy. Then he looked stricken, and I guessed he was thinking of my last words to him. And then some other emotion took the place of grief, something I found difficult to read; his eye hardened into an expression which I felt I ought to recognise . . . decision? Decision to kill me?

24

Edward had gone on staring at me even after Amy pulled on his arm. Apparently the missing member of their party had arrived. Still looking back at me, Edward disappeared with his party into the ballroom. I decided that he had tried to send me a wordless message to wait at the bar for him. I panicked. Picking up my purse, but forgetting to fetch a coat, I had fled into Market Square and wandered around trying to calm my nerves until I saw the lights of the shopping precinct through the alley.

Then . . . clunk!

It all fitted. I did represent a threat to Edward. It would harm his reputation if I broadcast my story. The gold heart he had given me dangled from my bracelet. He had seen me, recognised me, and must have followed me out of the hotel into the square. He had motive and opportunity, and he had incriminated himself by taking my bracelet. As to means, I didn't know what he'd used to hit me with . . . some tool from his car, perhaps? It didn't really matter.

What did matter was that he had my bracelet, and I wanted it back, not only because of the charms he and his friends had given me, but because of the years of happiness which were represented on it by the charms Pat had given me.

I considered sending a message into the ballroom that I wanted to speak to Edward, but decided against it. I was too shaken for a confrontation that night. I would telephone his house and leave a message. There was a public phone booth in the lobby. I went into the box and looked up Edward's number; he lived at a place called White Wings, just outside the city. I dialled, but there was no reply. I told myself that I wasn't thinking clearly. Naturally there was no reply, because all the Straker family would still be in the ballroom.

I put the phone back on its hook, and decided to get slightly tiddly before turning in. The bar was less crowded now, and the barman could attend to me without being distracted.

'Certainly, Mrs Neely,' he said, taking my order. 'Did Mr Straker catch up with you?'

'I spoke to Mr Jack Straker, yes.'

'Not Mr Jack. Mr Edward Straker, the one who's managing director of Coulsters Mills. He came in just after you left and asked me if I knew where you'd gone. I said I thought you'd gone out for a walk. Was that all right?' He gave me my drink. 'You are Mrs Neely, aren't you? I haven't made a mistake?'

'He asked for me by name? I've been away for many years. I don't think many people know my married name.'

'That's right. "Mrs Neely," he said. "Where's she gone?" And when I looked blank, he said, "Red hair, white dress". I felt sure he'd catch up with you.'

He'd caught up with me all right, I thought.

'Is he back in the ballroom now?'

26

'I suppose so. We've been very busy this evening. Afraid I didn't notice.'

Edward must have learned my married name from Con, because apart from Tom and Mary, no one else had kept in touch with me. Mary and Tom had their own small circle of friends which they did not seem to have enlarged much since the days I'd lived here. It was most unlikely that they would have come into contact with Edward socially, and even less likely that they would have spoken of me voluntarily. My parents were dead. I had no other contact with my past.

As I undressed and got into bed, I reflected that I must be going soft in the head. Edward had assaulted me, threatened me and stolen my bracelet, yet instead of calling the police I had covered up for him. I supposed that meant that I still loved him

I wished I'd never returned.

*   *   *

In the morning I ate a good breakfast and felt my fighting self take charge. I would be damned if I let Mary and Tom come between me and an understanding with my son. I would also be damned if I would let Edward drive me out of town. I would call his bluff; I would announce that I was going to buy a house, I would make plans for settling down, visit all my old friends . . . give Edward a scare. I

27

wasn't really going to expose him, but I was going to make him think that I might do so. Then, when he had returned my bracelet and grovelled for a while, I would retire to America and make a new life for myself there. Perhaps I'd take Johnny back with me, if we got on together.

The phone shrilled.

Edward. Immediately my breakfast began to disagree with me.

'Kit? I tried to catch up with you last night, but I must have missed you.'

I thought, yes, missed killing me!

'Kit, are you there? I want . . . that is, I would very much like ten minutes of your time.'

'Certainly,' I said, trying to think where it would be safe to meet him. There must be other people there, so that he couldn't try anything. 'Have coffee with me after lunch here in the hotel lounge. Two o'clock.'

A hesitation at the other end of the phone. He didn't like the rendezvous, but feared to argue in case I refused him an interview altogether.

'All right,' he said, and replaced his receiver.

I thought I'd handled that very well. The nerve of the man, ringing up like that after nearly nineteen years, and coming direct to the point without apology, or even enquiry as to my health! Then I grinned. Edward had never been any good at small talk.

The phone rang again, and this time it was Jack.

He was thrilled I was home again, wanted me to have lunch with him, to show me his new office premises and the home he and his wife had designed and built; he also wanted me to be guest at a Welcome Home party, and . . .

I arranged to drop by his office some time that morning. When he had finished, I phoned Con at St Luke's Vicarage. He was out, said his wife, but would be back later that morning. If it was urgent she could pencil me in for twelve o'clock. I said yes, it was urgent, and sallied forth to the bank.

The bank manager turned out to be another old friend, James Ferguson, nicknamed 'Morton' from some ancient tag about a one-time Chancellor of England who extorted money from people by saying, 'If you're spending money, then you must have some to spare for the king, and if you're not spending money, then you must be saving it, so how about some for the king!' Morton of Morton's Fork, they'd called him. Our Morton had been the treasurer of our group in the old days, collecting money for outings, organising transport and so on.

He stood up and gave me the Big Welcome act. 'Kit! Well, I declare! Someone said they'd seen you in the hotel last night. Married an American, didn't you? Over here to see the old folks?'

29

He was the man I'd half recognised in Edward's party the night before. I explained that yes, I'd married an American, and that he had recently died leaving me well provided for, and that I was thinking of returning to live in town, if I could find a suitable house. I had money in a bank in London, and would like it transferred back here, to his branch.

'Not for long, I'm sure,' he said gallantly, and then, realising that he'd phrased his compliment badly, he added, 'You'll be marrying again, that goes without saying.'

'Thanks, but no thanks. Pat's only been dead three months, and I'm not in the market for another husband.'

He smiled, but I could see him mentally totting up my assets—including my face and figure—and coming to the conclusion that The Little Woman wouldn't be allowed to run around loose with all that cash for long. I didn't tell him that I was no helpless Little Woman, because I have often found it very useful to pretend to be one. I can get my own way with men more quickly by pretending to be helpless than by a show of strength.

Morton fell over himself to arrange credit for me once he'd made a discreet call to London to verify my statement. He spoke enthusiastically of various big houses for sale in the neighbourhood, and I suggested he might like to spread the word that I was interested in buying. I wanted Edward—and everyone else for that matter—to know that I was no longer a penniless girl who could be bought off with a bundle of fivers.

Unwittingly, Morton supplied me with another piece of evidence against Edward. The Fergusons had voted the previous evening a failure because Edward had taken Amy home early, which had broken up their party. Edward had said that Amy had not been feeling well, but Morton thought she'd looked all right.

So far so good. I needed a car, so I took a taxi to Tinker's place. Tinker's name was really Timothy Mayhew, but everyone called him 'Tinker' because he spent all his time in or under old cars in the old days. It was Tinker who had relieved me of my virginity; or rather, he had forced me in spite of my protests. He was half cut at the time, and so ashamed of himself afterwards that he had offered to marry me. He'd been told that I was an easy lay, although he wouldn't say who had slandered me so. Some girl in the group, no doubt, jealous of the attention I attracted. I had refused to marry Tinker, but I continued to go out with him partly because he said he was madly in love with me, partly because he offered to teach me to drive, and partly because he was so adept in bed. Once I'd lost my virginity, I found I had a natural aptitude for sex which surprised me, and delighted Tinker.

Dear Tinker! Everything was black or white to him. He loved or disliked with intensity. He had been in the hotel the night before; I had seen him bustling through into the ballroom with another man and a woman, neither of whom I recognised. He was far too straightforward a character to attack me in the dark. If he wanted me out of town, he'd come straight out with it, and say so.

Con had written to tell me when Tinker had got married, and over the years I had accumulated other items of information about him. He had three children, I seemed to remember, and after his father's death Tinker had taken over the big garage at the end of Broad Street.

The garage was obviously doing well. It had a massive forecourt stocked with three sets of pumps, a shop for accessories, a shed for repairs and a yard at the side full of second-hand cars for sale.

I asked for Mr Mayhew, and a lanky lad of seventeen or so ambled up, the very image of what Tinker had been at his age. He even had Tinker's trick of sliding his hand along the coachwork of the car beside him, as if to assess the thickness of the paint. I asked for his father and was directed to an office where Tinker was sitting behind a big desk, amid a rash of pot plants.

Tinker looked hardly older than his son. His pleasure at seeing me again was muted in the

32

lad's presence, by his fear of what I might blurt out. I'd always liked Tinker in spite of our bad start, and I saw no point in worrying him. I said how marvellous it was to see him again, that he looked just the same, but that so much had happened to me in the intervening years that I felt like a different person.

He got the message, grinned and dismissed his son.

'Thought you'd married a millionaire,' he said. 'I went round to your old home once or twice, but your father told me you'd gone to stay with an aunt in London. The next we heard, you were married and in New York.'

My parents had told everyone who enquired for me that I had left town, whether I was sitting upstairs in my room crying, or doing the family wash in the kitchen. It was nice to think Tinker had remembered me.

'Pat was a good man,' I said. 'He thought I ought to come back here, buy a house, settle down. Do you think I'd like it, Tinker?'

'After America? Depends what you want, doesn't it?'

'I think I might like it. I wasn't sure until I got here, but the people in the hotel are so friendly, everyone is so friendly. Relaxed. You don't see people rushing about as you do in New York. I didn't realise before how tired I was. Nursing Pat, you know? We had nurses, of course, but I liked to be with him, and he liked me to be there . . . But I have a sister here, and one or two good friends. Enough for a start.'

'You can count on me, of course. That is . . .'

He gave me a sly grin, and flicked a finger at the photograph on his desk. His wife was a plump-faced, smiling woman. I wondered if Tinker was as randy as ever, and if his wife objected.

'I don't suppose you remember her,' he said. 'She used to admire you tremendously. She is much younger than me. If you do settle down here, I could fix it with her for you to come over to supper one night. She's a great cook.'

'I'd like that. She wasn't with you last night?'

He looked blank.

'I saw you going into the ballroom at the hotel. I'm staying there. I thought you might have seen me.'

'Wish I had. I was with my brother-in-law and his wife, and believe me, our party could have done with some livening up. The wife didn't feel up to it; some bug or other. There's a lot of it around at the moment.'

I said I was sorry, and could he find me a car to rent for a week or so. He was a good salesman, by which I mean that he wasn't out to rent me the most expensive car in his saleroom, but the one which would suit me best. As he waved me off, I reflected that Tinker was well in the clear. He had been wary of me, but not afraid.

34

Then I began to wonder why I was trying to turn up alternative suspects for the attack on me, when it was so obvious that Edward was the guilty party.

Fred Greenwood's estate agency was in Queens Street, at the other end of town to Mayhew's garage. I would have had difficulty finding a parking place if a helpful policeman had not shown me where to leave my car. Marvellous treatment, after New York.

Dear Fred. He had been the Billy Bunter of the group, the man who had introduced me to the delights of good food and wine. Under his tuition I had learned not to grimace when I swallowed oysters and chewed snails, and to appreciate dry wines and sherries. Like Paul, he had respected my virginity, and although he had taken it hard when I refused to marry him, he had given way to Tinker with good grace. It was true that he had also given me a gold charm—a sceptre—to hang on my bracelet, but I saw no reason why my return should alarm him.

Like Jack, he had recognised me in the hotel the previous evening, but unlike Jack he had done nothing about it. He had entered alone by the door near the ballroom, and looked around as if expecting to meet his wife.

Whom had he married? Shelia something? I couldn't put a face or a surname to her for the moment. He'd seen me, stood still for a moment with a shocked expression on his

35

heavy face, and then plunged through the doors into the ballroom. Like Paul, he had put on weight. Unlike Paul, he looked not exactly shabby, but certainly not well groomed. He reminded me of a great soft baby, whose mother had neglected to spruce up before sending out to play.

No, Fred wasn't pleased to see me. He was standing in the main office when I went in, and I could see his smile fade. I'd thought his reaction was odd the previous night, but now I was convinced my return had upset him in some way. He didn't invite me into his sanctum, even when I explained that I was in the market for a house with a big price-tag. He said gloomily that he had nothing which would suit me, and I'd better go elsewhere. I was on the point of asking him what the devil was the matter with him when a much older man, who turned out to be Fred's senior partner, spoke up.

'Mrs Neely, delighted to meet you! Something came in this morning which might interest you. Not on the open market yet, but if you want an unusual luxury house, White Wings might be just the thing.'

'She wouldn't be interested in that,' said Fred hastily. 'Far too big for you,' he continued, speaking to my collar-bone. 'Five bedrooms, two bathrooms, private lake, swimming pool, separate cottage for the staff, four acres of woodland . . . not at all the sort of

36

thing you were looking for, I'm sure.'

'Fred!' I said. 'Come off it! Likewise loosen up, will you? Do you mean that White Wings, Edward Straker's house, is on the market? And if so, why?' How ironic if I were able to buy Edward's house!

His telephonist interrupted before he could reply. 'Someone keeps ringing up for a Miss Jeffries, asking if she's arrived yet. We aren't expecting anyone of that name, are we?'

'That's me,' I said. I took the receiver from her, ill-prepared for what I was to hear.

'So you're there, are you?' the hoarse whisper said. 'You can't escape me. Be out of town by ten tonight, or die!'

TWO

'What is it?' Fred asked.

'A joker. Edward, I think. Threatening me. Telling me to get out of town or else . . .' I put a hand to my throat and dropped the receiver. I think it was the fact that Edward wasn't speaking in his normal voice which frightened me more than anything else. If he'd just said in a matter of fact way that he found my presence embarrassing, and that he'd do everything in his power to see I didn't stay, I'd have got the message.

Fred was dialling. He spoke to someone,

listened for a moment, killed the call, and tried twice more. Then he beckoned me into his office, bespoke some coffee and made me sit down.

'Edward is not at the hotel, or at the Mills. I tried White Wings on the off-chance, but he isn't there either. Cigarette?' He took one, but I refused. 'Look, Kit; you'll have to tell me what this is all about.'

He was himself again, the sweetest of Billy Bunters. I told him what had been happening, and the conclusions I had drawn. He heard me out, and shook his head.

'I'm sure it's not Edward. It's true that he left very early last night. They were hardly settled at table before they were whispering together, and then Edward fetched Piers, who was with some of his own friends, and they all went off together about fifteen minutes after they'd arrived. I could tell something had happened by the look on Amy's face. You know that prune look of hers? All pursed-up mouth. But why should he assault and rob you? Why should he want you out of town?'

This was getting difficult. I hadn't told Fred about Johnny, and I wasn't going to do so.

'Scandal?' I suggested.

'Ridiculous!' said Fred. 'Any man would be proud to have his name linked with yours. If I were you, Kit, I wouldn't take any notice of . . . Hey! That's a thought. If you had your bracelet stolen last night, then how come the

38

charm I gave you was returned to me this morning? It was pushed through the letter-box here. I thought you had returned it to me to show you didn't want me to presume on our old friendship, though heaven knows, it was innocent enough. It upset me, I can tell you.'

'I didn't send it back. I wouldn't have done so for the world. Whoever took it off me last night knew which charm you had given me, and sent it back.'

He didn't offer to give me the charm back, and since I'd lost all the others, I didn't ask for it.

'Edward wouldn't have bothered to send me back my charm,' said Fred. 'Such a petty action. He's not like that. He's generous with his time and his money. Yet . . . something is very wrong with him, I'll agree. He rang me first thing this morning before I'd left for work. He was at the Dragon Hotel, in the High Street. He said he and Amy had decided to separate with a view to divorce and he was putting White Wings on the market. It is his house, actually—nothing to do with her. I couldn't believe my ears when he said he wanted to sell it. He loves that place and is always working to improve it, putting in the swimming pool, building a studio for Piers. He said I should ring Amy to fix a date for measuring the house. He said he wanted me to find him a flat for the time being; something easy to run. Furnished, he said, because he

39

wasn't taking anything from White Wings. So I rang Amy, and much to my surprise she confirmed what he said about putting the house on the market, although she made out that they wanted something smaller now that Piers was eighteen and wanted to set up on his own. I didn't dare ask her whether it was true about the divorce, but I did check at the Dragon, and it's true that Edward booked in there last night. Amy told me to send someone out to measure the house tomorrow, after the dance. They're having a big "do" there tonight to celebrate Piers' eighteenth birthday. Everyone's going.'

Coffee came, and Fred asked me if I wanted to phone the police. I said no, not to bother, as I'd be seeing Edward later that day, and would sort it out then. Maybe he'd been overworking and ought to see a doctor.

'Shouldn't have thought you two had a lot in common,' said Fred, 'except good looks.'

'Not much,' I agreed. Except our need for each other, which was something I couldn't explain to Fred.

Fred sighed, relaxed in his outsize chair, reached for the biscuit tin and put on the look of a man brooding on a secret sorrow. I recognised the act, which I'd met everywhere I went, as being that of The Misunderstood Husband who wants to tell 'All' to Someone Sympathetic.

I liked Fred, and since I had just

remembered that his wife had definitely been called Sheila, I obliged.

'How is Sheila? It's three children you've got, isn't it?'

Of course, I ought to have known better. Three-quarters of an hour I sat there listening, nodding and shaking my head and saying, 'Oh, dear!' at intervals. But it did him good to talk. Poor Fred! Caught feeling up the *au pair*'s skirt, he had blustered instead of pleading guilty due to temporary insanity. Proceeding to a boozy party with a sense of injury, he ended up in a bedroom with a young girl who ought to have known better, and had been discovered, of course! Sheila had taken the three children and gone back to her parents, refusing to speak to him again. That had been six months ago and, according to Fred, Sheila now had an old flame hovering around her and the children could talk of nothing but their new Daddy, who took them to the zoo and sailing, and let them drink sherry in the evenings. Fred had tried weakly at first, and then with every bit of cunning that he possessed, to get Sheila back, but she wouldn't give him so much as the time of day. He was in a bad state, aware of what he had lost and that he had no one to blame for it but himself. He apologised for not speaking to me the night before, but he'd been feeling very nervous, having seen Sheila enter in another party just before him.

41

He perked up when I'd finished murmuring 'Poor Fred!' and offered to take me out to lunch, or if I was engaged for lunch, to dinner . . . but no, of course he had to go to Pier's party that evening. Tomorrow then?

I said maybe and left, glancing at my watch. I was going to be late for my appointment with Con.

I almost crashed into a light blue Mini as I drew away from Fred's place. The driver waved me on and followed me out of the city centre. He was still behind me when I reached Con's solid, creeper-clad vicarage.

Con's wife, Bet, came to the door and said not to worry about being late as Con hadn't got back himself yet, and would I care to have a sandwich lunch with him? She was a tall blonde, placid and beautiful, although her figure had thickened with the bearing of four children. I recognised her as the cousin of one of the lads I used to know. She had been Bet Hinds, hadn't she? She remembered me, of course, but she was poised enough not to resent me the way most women did. She knew my story and spoke of my problem sympathetically, adding that she had met my sister through some Women's Institute function, and that she believed Mary was going through a difficult time at the moment, what with the change of life and all. I asked Bet if she thought I ought to feel compensated for the loss of my child by all the money which Pat

42

had left me, and she said of course not, and that it was a pity I couldn't find some way of passing money on to Tom, as she had heard he wasn't doing too well financially.

It hadn't occurred to me that I could bribe Mary for access to my son. I told Bet I would have to think about it.

If Bet was more beautiful now than she had been as a teenager, Con's looks had not improved. He'd been an ugly, gangling youth with a prominent Adam's apple and a beak of a nose; his hair had always been untidy, and he was constantly mislaying the spectacles without which he was unable to read. The Reverend Conrad Birtwhistle was still untidy, ugly, bespectacled, late for every appointment, and luminous-eyed. Bet set a tray of sandwiches and coffee in the walled garden at the back of the vicarage and disappeared to do some shopping.

The vicarage garden was a much-used plot of land, filled with play equipment for the boys and a jumble of flowers in deep herbacious borders.

'Edward put those roses in for me,' said Con, eyeing a fine display of rambler roses along one wall, first with and then without his glasses. 'I'm hopeless in the garden, although Bet likes to mess around with a trowel. Jack put up the swing for the boys. Fred's godfather to the eldest, and it was he who gave them the cricket bats. It's made a mess of the lawn, I'm

43

afraid.'

'One big happy family,' I said.

'Which you are doing your best to upset.' He put his glasses back on, scrutinised me, sighed, smiled and hugged me. 'Dear Kit, forgive me for seeming churlish? I am very, very pleased to see you. You've hardly changed at all. A little older, perhaps even more beautiful. And no bracelet? Do you know, I felt as if you'd rejected me as a friend when I got the charm back this morning.'

'I didn't send it back. Someone stole my bracelet last night and seems to be returning the charms to their original owners. First Fred, and now you. It's worrying, because it must be someone who knew us very well. What is more, that same someone is trying to run me out of town. You are not the only one to disapprove of my return.'

'I didn't say that. I said that although I could see the idea of returning might appeal to you, it might be ill-timed from Johnny's point of view, and might not be acceptable to one or two other people. As indeed seems to be the case.' He sighed. 'You are a very strong person, Kit. You are the type who can create happiness for yourself wherever you go. You loved Pat, he is dead, and you need another man to love. All right. But did you really have to come back here to look for him?'

'Why not?'

'It depends whom you want, doesn't it? I

44

can't approve of divorce, you know.'

'You are jumping to conclusions!'

'Don't be angry with me, Kit. This whole affair has made me profoundly miserable. Everywhere I go, I meet someone who is disturbed by your return. Tears . . . I've never got used to coping with tears.'

'Who have I upset?'

'Jack for one. He's been very lonely since Liz died, but he was drifting into a good relationship with Marge Lawrence, who is a brave woman. She has two children who adore Jack. He's always wanted children. A marriage between Jack and Marge would have been very suitable and might well have come off if it hadn't been for your interference . . .'

'Interference!'

'Jack had a row and broke it off with Marge last night. I saw him in the street this morning and he could talk of nothing but you and how wonderful it was to have you back. Jack will ask you to marry him if you stick around.'

'And that would be a disaster?'

'Wouldn't it?'

'I suppose so.' I couldn't marry Jack, feeling as I did about Edward. 'All right. I'll make sure he doesn't hope for anything that way. I expect he'll go back to Marge eventually.'

'Not now he's marked the difference between you,' said Con. 'Then what about Fred, eh? I called in on Sheila just now, and she told me you'd been to see him and that he'd asked you to dine with him.'

'How on earth did she know that?'

'He telephoned her after you left. I suppose he was trying to make her jealous of you.' He munched a while. 'She was very jealous of you in the old days, I remember. Fred didn't do himself any good, of course, but he managed to upset her. I left her in tears, coward that I am!' He shook his head, trying to rid himself of the memory of Sheila's grief. 'Her mother was there, and told me to go, but I really do think I ought to have stayed. I'll ring Sheila in a little while and see if she's feeling better, offer to chauffeur her to Piers' party tonight.'

'Sheila . . . Ferguson,' I recalled. 'I couldn't place her at first. Morton's sister? Yes, I remember her hanging around once or twice when I was going out with Fred, and looking daggers at me. Oh, dear!'

'And don't tell me you mean to marry Fred, for I wouldn't believe you. As for the boy, the ostensible reason for your return . . .'

'Ostensible?'

'Don't you think you are being a little selfish, or at least, very self-centred? You come back here with your million-dollar clothes, flashing jewellery, with hands that haven't been near a kitchen sink for years, and disrupt the lives of all my friends with a carelessness that is almost criminal. Don't you care what damage you do, Kit?'

'All I've done is visit some of my old

friends . . .'

'And give them a glimpse of the unattainable, tantalise them into reaching for something they can't have. Johnny is well enough where he is. He is much loved, he is bright and cheerful and healthy and going to university this autumn if you don't throw a spanner in the works. He is the centre of Mary's life, and Tom's hope for the future. If he doesn't want to see you, then leave him alone. He doesn't need another mother, upsetting his established ideas and perhaps causing him to reject Mary because she is faded and tired and unfashionably dressed. He never asks about his father now. He doesn't seem to need him. He doesn't need your money, because it is better for his sort to make his own way in the world. He doesn't need you, Kit.'

Con ought to know. He'd been visiting Mary and Tom at regular intervals ever since I went to America. They didn't like what they termed his 'supervision' at first, but they'd grown to love him because he seemed to think of Johnny as his nephew. Con's letters to me had filled out the scrappy reports I had from my sister, and over the years he had been a true friend to me, and he had kept the secret of Johnny's parentage even from Mary. Even if he had not worn a dog-collar, I would have respected his judgement.

'Even if Johnny doesn't need me, I need

47

him. I feel . . . forlorn . . . without Pat.'

'I know. But my dear girl, don't you see that in your grief and your loneliness you are reaching out for what you want without thought of the consequences to other people? Go back to America. You are strong; you can remake your life. Keep yourself busy, that's the thing. Leave Edward alone.'

'I haven't contacted him. He's contacted me.'

'I know. He rang me this morning to tell me what he'd done. But, Kit, it's not too late to save him. 'You mustn't let him destroy himself.'

'You're talking nonsense!'

'Kit, my dear, I realise everyone doesn't feel as I do about the sanctity of marriage. In some cases it is wiser, I agree, for husband and wife to separate, but divorce . . . no. You've lived too long in a climate where a frequent change of partners seems to be the norm. Edward and Amy have been married for nearly nineteen years; they have much in common, and they have a son who is to succeed to the Coulster empire one day. I didn't know Edward too well in the old days, but we are good friends now. He has worked at his marriage, and he has worked at his job. Is he to throw it all away for a passing whim?'

'Why blame me for everything? You don't know what he did last night, do you? He . . .'

'Let me finish. You and Edward both seem

48

to confuse sex with love. When you let your desires take over before, you brought tragedy upon yourself, and this time the tragedy will hit Edward. He doesn't love Amy that way—all right! But he chose to marry her. I agree that there was a lot of pressure put upon him to do so, but there is little doubt in my mind that she loved him. Their marriage has endured. He has been faithful to her. Is she to be thrown aside after nineteen years of marriage, because she can't compete with you in the beauty stakes? And there is Piers; an intelligent lad, but nervy. He needs careful handling. His father understands and loves him. Piers is eighteen years old today and in the middle of a row about his future. Will you deprive the lad of his father at this crucial juncture? And what of Edward's home? White Wings means more to Edward than a house usually means to a man. Early and late he walks round the lake with his dog, tends his roses, potters in his greenhouse. He has achieved contentment. He delights in inviting his friends' children to play tennis on his courts, and punt on his lake. Four times a year he opens his grounds for charity. He is very active in the Boys' Club that he's started down by the Mills. He has grown into his setting.'

'I didn't expect material arguments from you.'

'Here's another. Amy and her family own Coulsters Mills. Edward has some shares—I don't know how many, but not enough for control. He has a contract as managing director, which means they could throw him out if he displeased them. How will he make a living if he divorces Amy? He is used to a Rolls-Royce, hand-made shirts, and servants by now remember! You are going to destroy him, Kit. You want to take away his reputation, his son, his, home, and his job.'

I cried out. He held my hand, suffering with me.

'All right,' I said at last. 'I'll go away again. I was to have seen Edward this afternoon, but I'll leave a message at the hotel to say I can't keep the appointment. As for Johnny, will you see him for me and find out if he really wishes me to leave him alone? I'm not even sure that Mary has told him whose son he is. I asked her to do so on his eighteenth birthday, but she was so evasive when I saw her . . . it would be like her to refuse him the information and it is only fair that he should know. Fair to Edward as well as to Johnny. Will you do what you can for me, too? I could come back here . . . no, not here! I could manage a visit to London at Christmas, say. Johnny could meet me there without upsetting Mary. Oh God, give me some hope for the future!'

He held me tightly until I was in control once more. Luckily when I cry it doesn't make my eyelids puff up. I got out my powder compact and dabbed at my nose. Con mopped his eyes and blew his nose, blaming his hay fever. He'd mislaid his glasses by that time, and I had to help him find them.

Although I managed a smiling farewell, I was shaking so hard I found it difficult to put the key in the ignition of my car, and my driving was somewhat erratic. I'm afraid I gave one or two drivers cause to curse women before I got back to the Square, in particular a man in a pale blue Mini, who nearly rammed me at one intersection. I thought I recognised him, and therefore raised my hand in greeting, but when he scowled at me I realised I must have been mistaken. I parked in the Square opposite the hotel, and the Mini parked nearby. A fawn-coloured Rolls with an ES number plate stood in front of the hotel; Edward had arrived. The windows of the hotel lounge overlooked the Square, so he must have seen me. I could find a public phone box and ring the hotel with a message for him to the effect that I couldn't make our date. I could, but I wouldn't. I wouldn't run away, and besides, I wanted my bracelet back.

He rose as I entered, and indicated a chair beside him. He had been sitting in the bay-window overlooking the Square, reading *The Times*. Coffee for two was waiting on a table for him. He looked very big and well-groomed; exactly the way I liked a man to look.

I sat down, or rather my knees bent and deposited me on the chair. I clasped my hands

51

over my handbag so that he wouldn't see I was trembling. My conscience was warning me that I ought to keep this interview short and formal, but my heart was saying, 'Take him— he's yours!'

'Will you pour out?' said Edward. 'Half and half for me.'

He seemed to be feeling the strain, too. He fidgeted with his paper, laid it on his knee, removed it when it threatened to slip to the floor, and finally sent it skimming at an empty chair nearby. It missed and fell on the floor. We both looked at it, but he made no move to pick it up.

'I'm sorry I'm late,' I said. It was just after two.

'I was early.' He cleared his throat. Far from threatening me, Edward was as nervous as I was. He fidgeted with something in his breast pocket, withdrew it and laid it on the table in front of me. A deposit account book for one of the larger building societies.

'Johnny is not with you?' he asked. 'I hoped he might be. I asked at Reception, but they said you were alone. I suppose he's at one of the excellent summer camps they run in America?'

I didn't reply. Conflicting notions rushed through my mind; that Edward was not behaving as he would have behaved if he had attacked me, that he had no idea I'd left Johnny behind when I'd gone to the States, and that his hair was not fairer than it used to be, but fast turning grey. Suddenly I was as convinced of his innocence as I had been sure of his guilt before I saw him.

'Well, never mind that,' he said. 'Would you arrange for him to get this money? I'll give you a cheque for it. I believe you are fairly well off, but a boy of eighteen can always do with some extra money. I started putting it into the building society as soon as I heard about him.'

I opened the book and looked at the total, which was startlingly high. It occurred to me that this was exactly the sort of thing which Pat might have done under the circumstances. It also occurred to me that Edward was now forty-two years old, which was the age Pat had reached when I met him.

'Does he know about me?' said Edward. 'I would like him to know, if you don't object. Does he take after you? I don't even know what he looks like. Con wouldn't . . .'

'Con! It was he who told you my married name, and he who has been giving you information about me?'

'Only since I found out. He made me promise not to contact you, and in return he gave me news of you and the boy, twice a year. Just that you were both well, or that Johnny had had measles. I kept my promise, but I asked a business contact of mine to check up on your husband for me, to find out if he was in a good position financially. I thought you

53

might be in need, even though Con said you weren't. My friend goes over to the States three or four times a year on business. He said he'd made enquiries about your husband, and you were all right. I didn't learn of your husband's death until last week. Thursday. I've already told Con I consider that absolves me from my promise not to contact you.'

Something didn't add up. The first entry in the building society's book was for three years after Johnny's birth and my departure.

I said, 'But I phoned your old home when I knew I was pregnant. Your father took the call and promised to tell you I wanted to speak to you urgently.'

'My father had a vested interest in my marriage. He said nothing to me about your call.'

'I wrote.'

'I found the letter three years later, when I was sorting through some old papers.'

'But I got a letter from you enclosing money.'

'So Con told me. I didn't write it. You've never seen my writing, have you?' He took some papers from his pocket and fanned them out on the table. 'Can you identify the handwriting from these?'

I pointed to one. 'That's it, I think.'

'That's mine,' he said, pointing to another sample. 'Have you got that letter with you?'

'No, its in a safety deposit box in New York.

54

I suppose your father intercepted my letter, and wrote to me, signing your name. He said horrible things.'

'He's dead. But if you'd only waited, and contacted me in person . . . phoned me again . . .'

'What would you have done? Thrown over Amy for me? I'm not a fool, I know you wouldn't.' I lifted the coffee-pot and tried to pour out. My hand trembled so much that I spilt coffee on the tray. I put the pot down, on the verge of tears.

'You are right, of course.' His voice was as harsh as his words. He inspected his right hand, which was also shaking. Setting his jaw, he steadied his hand, picked up the coffee-pot, balanced it, and poured out for both of us, filling both cups to the brim.

'Triumph of mind over matter,' he remarked, and then, comically, 'I forgot to leave room for the cream! Can you drink it black? I don't think I could pour it back!'

'Don't tempt providence! Let's pretend we didn't want any!'

He laughed, meeting my eyes for the first time. 'That's what I loved about you, your gifts of kindness and laughter.'

'I wasn't kind to you.'

'Did I deserve that you should have been? I ruined you. It was no thanks to me that you married well afterwards.'

'I hurt you. I've always regretted saying what

I did.'

'It was the truth. Truth often hurts. I admit I didn't get much joy out of sex after that, remembering . . .'

I opened my handbag and sought for my handkerchief. 'It wasn't true,' I said, blowing my nose, 'I was just being catty.'

'It was the truth. You looked me straight in the eye when you said it. If you have to lie, you always turn away and mumble—just as you are doing now, to save my feelings. Besides, Amy has always agreed with you.'

I wanted to say that I wouldn't mind hopping into bed with him that very moment, but I wasn't sure he would wish to do so.

'Johnny!' he said, reminding himself of the purpose of this interview. He'd obviously rehearsed what he wanted to say, and was going to get it out come what may. 'I'd like to meet him, if you don't object. I could fly over at Christmas time for a few days, or if he'd like to visit England, maybe I can find somewhere decent to live before then . . .'

'You really are going to sell your home?'

'It's the price I have to pay for a divorce. I can't keep White Wings and pay Amy half its value.'

'Not because of me, surely?'

'Yes.'

'One look in a mirror?'

'One look was enough before, wasn't it? I fell in love with you the first time I saw you, but it was too late. Three months too late. Then you disappeared . . . perhaps you were wise because I'd have pursued you otherwise; once Piers was born Amy had little use for me in bed. But there was the Works, and my son, and later on there was White Wings; there was no point in breaking with Amy while your husband was alive, although I've had enough evidence to divorce her for nearly five years. She's got a lover—a hair-stylist here in town. She does not wish to use him as a replacement for me, you understand; he is an extra. I suppose I ought to have objected more strongly when she took him on, but there have been so many arguments . . . disagreements about things I felt strongly about. The fault was mine, in that I did not care sufficiently one way or the other.'

'But she does not wish to lose you.'

'It takes two . . .! She cannot keep me. As for Piers, I said they would make him a director of the Mills on his eighteenth birthday over my dead body, and they have done so. He is not ready for it yet, but . . . he will not listen to me any longer. Also he inherits a large sum from a trust fund set up by his grandfather today, and he doesn't even need to draw on me for money any longer. I'm as free now as I'll ever be. Not free of guilt, of course, or remorse . . . and as you know, I'm not much good to a woman in bed. Crippled, but free, as you might say.'

'You mustn't destroy yourself. There's your position at the Mills . . .'

'Yes and no. If they sack me, I'll get compensation; but I don't think they will sack me because they will find it difficult to get a replacement who is capable of doing the job so well. I'm young enough to start again somewhere else, and I'm told my talents are rated high on the labour market. I shan't be able to afford another White Wings for some time, but I'll build another house somewhere, and it will become as dear.'

'You mean you've thought it all out and that nothing I say or do will influence you?'

'I wouldn't say that. A man doesn't often get a second chance at happiness. If you are not already committed, then I shall do my best to win you.'

'You mean you want to climb into bed with me again?'

'I mean marriage, if you'll have me, knowing that I'm a poor bargain. Don't flirt with me, Kit. You knew I meant to try when you saw me in the mirror last night. You gave yourself away. Admit it!'

'Just unfinished business. Then why not hop into bed with me and get it out of your system?'

'That was an offer!' remarked Edward the business man.

He took my chin in his fingers and forced me to look up at him. I could feel my face

58

redden. He released me, opened the lid of the coffee-pot, emptied half the contents of the cups back in, helped us both to milk and sugar, and handed me my cup. He had recovered his nerve.

'Jumping into bed with you would be all right for today,' he said, 'but what about tomorrow and the day after? I want exclusive rights. I want all my dreams come true, in and out of bed.'

I sipped at my coffee and set it down. It was cold. I pulled the sugar basin towards me and started playing with the spoon. He took it off me, and possessed himself of my hands.

'Well, Kit?'

I pulled one of my hands free, and ran it over the gold bracelet of his watch. I unbuttoned his shirt cuff, inserted my fingers between the fine cotton and the smooth skin on the inside of his arm . . . and curving my fingers, I drew my nails lightly, over it. He drew in his breath. He lowered his head. He couldn't move, and he didn't know where to look.

Satisfied, I rebuttoned his shirt, smoothed down the fine cloth of his sleeve, and put my hand over his.

'It seems to me that you have everything that a woman might want,' I said. 'I'll marry you the moment you're free.'

'More coffee, sir?' asked the waiter.

I was uneasily happy. When the waiter interrupted us, Edward recalled that he had an important meeting at three o'clock, and we walked out together to his car. I had so much to tell him, about Johnny, and the attack on me, and Pat . . . then there was the promise I'd made Con, and the problem of Jack to be dealt with. Which should I speak of first, and when? Edward had said that much to his distress he could not see me again that day. He had promised Amy he would attend Piers' party at White Wings that night, and he felt he ought to go.

He held my arm tightly. Everyone could see we were in love. Happiness had loosened his tongue, and he laughed aloud.

'Do you realise this is the first time I've gone anywhere in public with you? Just walking across the square like this . . . I can hardly believe I'm awake. I've day-dreamed so many years, made so many plans for leaving Amy and put them off for another couple of months because there was Piers to be considered, and I was putting in a sprinkler system in the gardens, and there were the boys at the Club; I didn't want to let them down, and besides, I've grown very fond of one of them. You won't mind if I continue to go down there now and then, will you? And there's my dog. Crisp is his name. Not a suitable name for a dog, but Piers called him that. I've had to leave him with the gardener for the moment. He doesn't think much of women usually. To think I hesitated to leave Amy because you might not take to Crisp, or he to you! To think I might have gone on day-dreaming and doing nothing about it if I hadn't seen you . . . I did plan to go to New York when I heard about your husband's death, but then I wasn't sure you'd want to see me . . .'

For a moment I found it difficult to breathe. Con had spoken the truth. Edward would not have left Amy and thrown up his job, his son and his beloved home if I hadn't nudged him into action.

I couldn't go through with it. We had confused sex and love, that was all. For a half-hour of purple passion, Edward was prepared to throw away everything he valued. He had moved away from reality into his land of day-dreams, and it was up to me to rescue him.

He checked his watch, swinging me round to face him, delighting in the exercise of his superior strength. Then he saw my face and released me. His eyelids contracted. He knew he was about to get hurt.

'I was just thinking,' I lied, picking a bit of fluff from his jacket, 'how much I'm looking forward to showing you off to all my New York friends.' It would do no good to tell him that I didn't love him. I would have to strike more subtly, at his pride. 'I know what they'll

61

say, that you attract women with money! After all, it must help to know that by leaving Amy you won't be any worse off, financially. You'll just love my little apartment in New York, although it isn't usually a good idea to have pets in a flat, as I'm sure you know. Besides, they mess the place up with their hairs and their feeding bowls. You could have Pat's study, and after a while I'll find you a post in one of the companies he used to own—I'm sure they'll find something for you if I ask nicely, though of course it wouldn't be anything like your present job . . . but then, I'd have you all to myself, all the time . . . no need for you to work any more when you're my husband . . .'

'New York?' He took my hand and tried to make me face him, but I dived into my handbag for my compact and started to powder my nose.

'Why, of course. You don't really expect me to settle down here, in this crummy old place which doesn't even have a decent dress shop!' I managed a light laugh. 'Don't be ridiculous, my sweet! I'm used to a certain standard of living. No housework, for a start. Maids, and a chauffeur, and my own bathroom. That's an absolute minimum. I've got plenty of money, but I'm not laying it out to buy an inferior house in this neck of the woods.'

I didn't dare look at him. I frowned, turning on my heel to look round the Square. I felt like an executioner.

'It's not going to work, is it?' I said, addressing the sky. Out of the corner of my eye I saw him shake his head. 'We were stupid to think it would work, Edward. There's too much against it. We're both too set in our ways to change, and although your offer was very flattering, I'm glad we didn't get any further than having a cup of coffee together. Give Con a cheque for Johnny's money, and he will pass it on. Off you go to your meeting!'

He didn't move. I conquered an impulse to throw my arms round him and turned away, leaving him standing beside his car. I walked back to the hotel. On the steps I turned to wave goodbye. He was still standing there, looking at the spot where I'd been. I went in.

The receptionist gave me some letters and I asked him to book me a room at the Dorchester for that night. I said I'd been called back to New York unexpectedly, and would they please prepare my bill, and have some brandy sent up to my room.

My bedroom window overlooked the Square. Edward and his car had gone.

I had torn him to pieces all right, but I'd done the same thing to myself. I kept saying, out loud, as if to convince myself, that I had done the right thing, and that Edward would go back to Amy and Piers and his dog and White Wings and everything would be just the same for him as before. I argued that he would be happier in the future because I had destroyed his daydream.

My mental pain was so great that I couldn't sit down, but charged around the bedroom packing, bumping into furniture, dropping things, brushing my hair, anything to keep on the move . . .

For underneath the arguments I had used against marriage to Edward, there was another argument going on; that Edward was old enough to know exactly what he was doing, and that I'd no right to try to twist his life back into its old course by a trick. I didn't give a damn where I lived or how much my clothes cost, and I quite liked cooking. It was true that I'd been used to having a bathroom of my own, but the thought of sharing one with Edward made me feel dizzy with joy. It was very possibly true that Edward would have delayed making the break with Amy if I had not returned, but now that I had, I feared the damage was done for good. He wouldn't have spoken so freely of his doubts if he hadn't overcome them. If Edward did not return to Amy, had I hurt myself and him for nothing? I tried to recall Con's arguments, but grew confused. If Edward left Amy but did not marry me, what would happen to his job, his house and his son?

Surely this agony could not be endured for nothing!

I ripped open the letters that had been

waiting for me in the hotel; a note from Fred asking me to have lunch with him on the morrow, three letters from New York . . . I must remember that New York was 'home'! . . . and a packet containing eighteen battered gold charms. They were the ones Pat had given me, still recognisable but no longer fit to hang on a bracelet. It looked as if someone had taken a hammer to them.

The phone rang.

'Did you get the package I sent you?' enquired the hoarse whisper. 'You'll get the same treatment yourself if you don't clear out.'

'Oh, I'm going.'

'Make sure you do. There's a train every hour on the hour. To show that we mean business, we've fixed your car for you.'

The phone went dead. I put it down and went to the window to see if I could locate my car, which was standing opposite. It looked all right to me, but even as I watched, a puff of metal ballooned up from the bonnet, followed by the sound of an explosion. Passers-by screamed and cowered against nearby buildings. Flames? No. Yes. Police whistle. Someone running out of the Square. More screams, children wailing, parents clutching them.

Oh, God. What have I done?

THREE

The phone rang. It was the receptionist, saying that Mr Straker had arrived to see me, and was asking if he might come up to my room.

'Who?' It couldn't possibly be Edward, could it?

'Mr Jack Straker,' said the receptionist. 'He's anxious about you, wants to be sure you weren't hurt in the bomb incident.'

Incident. I only caused it, I didn't get hurt in it.

'Is anybody hurt?' I asked.

No one had been hurt, they thought, only shocked. And no damage seemed to have been done except to the car. They said the owner would get a shock when he came back. So no one knew that it was my car.

Jack knocked and came in, carrying a sheaf of carnations. He was relieved to find I was still in one piece, but upset to see me crying. Before he could say anything, I asked if he'd find the brandy I'd ordered some time ago. The hotel staff were very pleasant, but not as efficient as those in New York. He thrust the carnations into my arms and went off, muttering about 'damned IRA frightening the life out of the women'.

I wondered what I'd do with the carnations. I supposed I could take them back to

London with me, to cheer up my room at the Dorchester. I had returned to my packing when Jack came back with my drink.

'What are you packing for? I thought you were back for good.' He thrust a drink at me. 'Come on—drink up and tell your Uncle Jack what's gone wrong!' I shook my head. 'Have I done something? Said something stupid? Come on, love! Tell us why you sent me back my gold charm, at any rate!'

'I didn't. Someone stole my bracelet last night, and is returning the charms to their original owners.' I thought it was odd that Edward hadn't mentioned getting his charm back. I could now acquit him of responsibility for the attack on me, which left me without any clue as to the identity of my assailant. It didn't matter now. Nothing mattered.

'What the devil would anyone do that for?' asked Jack. He was peering out of the window, half his attention on what was happening in the Square. 'The police have arrived . . . they'll soon sort it out. Is it the car bomb which has upset you, Kit? Surely not. You've more sense than to let that worry you. I thought you were staying, and that we could have some fun together, like old times.'

'You have your own friends . . . Con, Fred, Marge. I'm sorry Liz died, but . . .'

'Is it Marge that's worrying you? She's fine as a friend and marvellous as a business partner, but there's nothing else in it.'

67

'Would she say the same thing about you?'

He looked uncomfortable, and then stuck his jaw out, just like his brother. 'Maybe she did think it might work out. Maybe I thought it might, too. We jogged along merrily enough but somehow I've never been able to ask her to marry me although I'd dearly love to take her kids over. When I saw you last night I suddenly realised how dreary I'd been feeling ever since Liz died. I'd felt that nothing was worth bothering about, you know? Hardly able to crawl around at work . . . helping Morton with his charities in the evenings to keep myself occupied. Hospital visiting . . . helping Edward with his Boys' Club. There was no fun in it. I was living a half-life without excitement or gaiety. I looked at Marge last night after we'd met you, and, I thought, I'm not dead yet, and I'm under no compulsion to propose to you. If I'd been sixty plus and looking for a spot of quiet companionship around the gas fire, maybe I'd have been able to settle for Marge, but I'm not sixty—I'm not yet thirty-five—and I'm damned if I'll settle for second best.'

I sat on the bed and howled. Jack knew what to do. He put an arm round my shoulders, handed me a handkerchief, and said, 'There, there!' every now and then. I respond to that sort of treatment. It occurred to me that I could tell Jack everything, without fear of it going any further.

'It's Edward, isn't it?' he asked, forestalling

me. 'I saw you in the Square a while back, arm in arm.'

I peeped at him over the edge of his handkerchief. He looked sorry for me, but not stricken with jealousy.

'Did you know?'

'I knew he was mad about you years ago, but I wasn't sure how you felt about him. He made it obvious, didn't he, the way he used to watch you! The story got around that you dropped out of sight when he got married, which was why I never looked you up, afterwards. I thought you wanted it that way.'

'And you'd met Liz by that time!'

He grinned. 'There was that! Dear Kit, why the tears? You have my whole-hearted approval of the match.'

'You forget—Edward is already married.'

'Who could forget the gorgeous Amy!' He pulled a face. 'Brother Edward never complains, because our old man drummed it into him that it is a sign of weakness to do so, but I don't like to see dumb animals suffer . . . not that Edward is quite as dumb as he used to be, and Amy certainly doesn't get everything her own way, but you get my meaning?'

'I thought you two hated each other, but you sound as if you cared about him.'

'In my callow youth I was jealous of Edward because he was the old man's pet, and he was so strong and handsome whereas I was . . . quite the opposite. Then one day I found out who had paid for me to train as an architect, and I had to revise my opinion of him.' He pulled another face. 'Didn't you know, sweetheart? Our old man was the original improvident fool. He was in debt up to his eyelids and threatened with bankruptcy and worse, from which he was saved by my brother's falling in the Coulsters' way. Oh, ho! says Mr Coulster; here's a pretty young boy who'll not only keep Amy happy, but also keep the Mills afloat for another generation. Our old man gets his debts paid off, money is forthcoming for my training, and Edward gets a life sentence.'

'He said he had to marry her, but I didn't understand why.'

' "Come into my parlour," she said, and at first he went willingly. You know how we were brought up, Kit. No affection, no laughter. Amy is a clever girl. Edward was starving for affection, and she gave it to him. He had no money, and she was the richest girl in town. She talked of making him her prince . . . yes, really! I overheard her and laughed myself silly, but it was foolish of me, for a concern as big as Coulsters Mills is the modern equivalent of a Ruritanian kingdom, isn't it? She bought him presents, which no one had done since Mother died. She foretold a brilliant future for him, and hung on his every word. She induced her relations to welcome him. She dazzled him. He proposed willingly enough.

Why wouldn't he? It was a fantastic opening for a young man without prospects or money, and, you see, they made it clear that the traffic wasn't one way, and that they valued him for what he could give them. And they were right! Edward would have gone to the top in any field, and the Coulsters were lucky to latch on to him when he was just starting. God, how terrified they were when he tried to back out! I can remember the fuss very clearly, although at the time I didn't understand what it was all about. I was thought too young and heedless to be included in the family councils, but I was able to put the pieces together later. Amy doesn't care what she says when she's in a bad temper, and our old man went all pathetic in his old age and told me the rest . . . wanting to justify his actions, I suppose.'

'What did happen?'

'Everyone put pressure on Edward to go through with the marriage. He was threatened with being blacklisted, promised shares in the Mills, our old man said he'd commit suicide . . . and when none of those things brought him to heel, Amy told Edward that she was pregnant.'

'Don't be daft. Piers is eighteen today, but Johnny's birthday fell six weeks ago, so she couldn't have been pregnant when he made love to me.'

'I didn't say she *was* pregnant. I said she told him she was. Subtle distinction. Got him to marry her under false pretences, if you ask me. Who's Johnny?'

'My son by Edward. Edward didn't even know he existed for several years, but he wants to acknowledge him now. It happened after you left for university.'

It was a shock to him. He blinked, recovered, and demanded that I tell him everything. I did, even down to my determination to leave town so that the evil I had brought on everyone might die down.

Jack listened without interruption, his face reflecting his concern over each facet of my story with rapid changes of expression. Unlike Edward, Jack was bad at concealing what he felt; later on that day I met someone else with the same mobility of feature, and was strongly reminded of him.

'Catalyst!' he exclaimed, when I had finished. 'You're not evil, and you're off-balance to think that you are. The evil and the hatred were here before, damped down and therefore twice as vicious. You are the catalyst, that's all. Your presence has given us all a little push, made us reassess existing situations, old relationships; like me and Marge. You aren't responsible, because you didn't will any of this to happen. It's silly to blame yourself for my breaking with Marge, and as for feeling guilty about it—well, why should you? I knew you wouldn't marry me . . . well, perhaps it did cross my mind that I might ask you, but I probably wouldn't have done so. No! That's a lie. I did mean to ask you. Marge charged me with it last night, and I told her I would marry you, if you'd have me. I'd forgotten about Edward, and that he might have a prior claim on you until I saw you both together in the Square just now. It shook me, I can tell you. There, there! Not to cry! I went and had a drink and told myself there was no harm done, and that I'd come and congratulate you, and ask you to find me someone just as nice as you so that we could have a double wedding . . .!'

'What nonsense you talk!' But his arm was comforting around me.

'I'm glad you've come back. I was living in a land of dreams, comparing every woman to Liz and therefore unable to form a new relationship, even with Marge. Self-deception. I'll tell you something else. I liked you a lot in the old days—who wouldn't?—but I had another motive for taking you out, and that was to spite Edward. There I was, waltzing around with you, and my brilliant elder brother, who was the apple of Father's eye, engaged to the richest girl in town, and had a golden future, was grinding his teeth in envy of me. Do you hate me for it, Kit?'

I shook my head. I could understand how he'd felt. After all, hadn't I gone out with him because he was the nearest thing I could get to Edward?

'I've promised Con I won't harm Edward,

73

and I've managed to put him off me for good. Dear Jack, do try to understand!'

'I understand more than you think, my girl. What, is Edward made of paper that he should fear to lose his job and that white elephant of a house? I know him better than you do. We signed a peace treaty years ago and I'd say we've been pretty good friends these last few years; especially since Liz died.' He moved restlessly, releasing me, as sorrow hit him once more. 'If Edward got the sack tomorrow he'd be offered half a dozen equivalent positions by the end of the week. You don't seem to understand how big a name he's become. As for Piers . . .' Jack threw out his arms in defeat. 'Edward has tried to instil some sense into the lad, and failed. He's spoilt rotten, thinks only of money; a typical Coulster. Edward has had to fight Amy to bring the boy up straight, but . . . by the age of eighteen the fight is won or lost, isn't it?'

'Does Piers know about me? Could he have resented me on his mother's behalf, and on his own . . . enough to do something about it?'

'Like attack you? I have never heard him speak your name. Come to think of it, I've never heard Edward speak of you, either. It would depend on what Amy had told him, if anything. As to attacking you—yes, I think he might if he thought you represented a threat to him, but he'd have to be sure he could get away with it.'

74

'What does he look like?'

'Tall, fair-haired, handsome. Like Edward in looks but finer drawn. Like Amy in everything else. He could have attacked you. He left early, with Amy and Edward. Drove his mother back, I think. Edward took the Rolls, collected some things from the house and ended up at the Dragon. But then, lots of people left around the same time. Fred and Sheila had words and departed forthwith—separately. Marge stormed out after the scene with me. I came in search of you, but you'd disappeared by that time. Let's go and take a look at the scene of the crime, shall we?'

I took him out into the Square. A number of people were now hanging around the wreck of my car. What ought I to do about it? They would trace it to Tinker at some point, I supposed, and although I could reimburse him for the damage, he would have to tell the police that I had rented it from him, and then they would want all sorts of details from me, which would drag all my friends into the filthy business. I explained this to Jack, who said that nevertheless it was my duty to tell what I knew.

'This it?' Jack paced the passageway. At the moment it was full of people hurrying to and fro between the Square and the shops beyond. We re-enacted the attack on me. Jack stood in for my unknown assailant, and then asked whether I could make a guess about relative heights.

'About the same height as you,' I said. 'Which rules out Edward and Paul, who are taller. It also rules out poor Fred, who is so much larger.'

'That's a blow,' said Jack. 'Because it also rules out Piers, and I sometimes think I'd like to see my nephew in the dock. Take him down a peg.'

I hoped he was joking, but feared he was not. 'You're not going to see anyone in the dock. I told you, I'm leaving.'

'Their lucky day . . . night, rather!' He pointed to the one and only light fitment in the alley, in which the bulb was broken. 'The alley was dark, there was some piping to hand . . .' He pointed to where workmen were digging a hole in the Square, fenced around with metal poles. 'Only, if it was a spur-of-the-moment affair, why take the coat from the hotel? It's only that fact which doesn't fit my theory. I think maybe I will have a casual word with Piers tonight about dark alleys and bracelets; see if he looks self-conscious. Shall we go?'

'Where?'

'To see your son Johnny, of course. He's also my nephew, and I'm not missing out on a relationship like that. You don't think he'd like to be an architect, do you? I've got a practice all ready to hand on eventually, and enough money for two . . .'

'But, Jack, I told you that Mary and Tom won't even listen . . .'

'Poor souls! I bet they're scared stiff of you, with no legal hold on their blue-eyed boy.'

'No legal . . .?'

'You said they didn't adopt him. Legally he's John Jeffries. Of course, when you marry Edward he'll be legitimised and I suppose he'll become Edward's heir. Piers comes into all the Coulster money as a matter of course. And don't tell me you hadn't thought about the legitimacy angle!'

He opened the door of a good-looking Citröen and pushed me inside.

'I am not marrying Edward,' I said firmly.

'I wouldn't be too sure about that, if I were you. Edward has a way of getting what he wants. If he doesn't tumble to it that Con has tried to choke you off, I'll tell him myself. I'll be seeing him tonight at the dance.'

'I'll be gone by then.'

'Then he'll come after you.'

'No, he won't. He'll accept the situation. Coming after me would entail too great a break with his world. I admit that if I did stay, and made myself available, he'd be tempted . . . Jack, you're going too fast! How could I have forgotten what a terrible driver you are? I want to arrive in London in one piece tonight!'

Jack laughed, but slowed down, asking for directions to Mary's place. I obliged, and then went back to worrying about my blown-up car, and Tinker, who was about Jack's height and might well have . . .

Nonsense. One good thing; Jack seemed to have forgotten about my making a report to the police.

Mary and Tom lived in a quiet, tree-lined street of old-fashioned detached houses. Although Tom was a builder, his house had a neglected air. Mary was in the front garden, weeding, and a big-boned girl with long brown hair in a pigtail was mowing the lawn for her.

'Jesus Christ!' swore Jack as he parked the car. 'Will you look at the way that woman holds herself! I'd like to dress her in a golden caftan, with her hair wound round her head.'

He was staring at the brown-haired girl, whom I now saw was no girl, but a woman in her early thirties. It didn't look to me as if she ever bothered with make-up, or nail varnish, or good clothes. She was a nice-looking girl, but nothing special. The sort of woman who usually detested me on sight.

Mary saw me, and stood up. The brown-haired woman stopped mowing the lawn and stretched, with her arms high above her head. She wasn't wearing a bra. She was taller than Jack would be, but, as he said, she was magnificently built. She half-smiled, seeing us, and lifted an eyebrow in Mary's direction to find out whether her friend wished her to disappear now that visitors had arrived.

'Don't go, Hazel,' said Mary, her pretty voice flattened into a monotone. Her eyes were on Jack, not me. 'These people are not staying.'

'Good afternoon, Mrs Blake,' said Jack, offering his hand. 'I'm Jack Straker. I've only just heard about Johnny, and all I can say is that I wish I'd known about him all along.'

'Get out!' Mary struck at his hand and backed away.

'Don't be silly, Mary,' I said. I felt deathly tired, but now that we were there, I supposed we had to go through the motions. I could see that Mary was not open to argument. There was no car standing in the garage, so Tom must be out. The house looked blank. I was sure that Johnny wasn't in.

'What is it?' Jack asked me. 'Does she think I'm the boy's father?' Then to Mary. 'I wish I were. I'm his uncle, you see. Come now— let's be sensible. Maybe you can ensure that Kit doesn't see the boy if she's only here for a few days, but you can't stop me making his acquaintance because I live here and now that I know about him, I can make contact with him any time I wish.'

Mary's eyes were wild. I don't think she understood half of what Jack had said. I tried to touch her. She turned and ran into the house. The brown-haired woman hesitated, and then asked Jack if he thought she should go after Mary. It was interesting that she should turn to Jack for information. While Jack started to explain that he thought it would be best if I talked to my sister alone, I ran after

79

Mary through the dark hall into the kitchen. She was taking some pills. Tranquillisers, I suppose. Poor Mary.

Unasked, I sat down at the kitchen table.

I enquired where Tom and Johnny might be. She didn't reply. She was crying. Her hair was untidy and she wore an ancient apron over a print dress that had seen better days. She was plainer than ever, and not for the first time I wondered how our parents had come to produce two such very different children. No wonder we had never been able to talk easily to each other. I wondered what she would say if I offered to put money into Tom's business in exchange for the right to see my son.

I asked if I might have a cup of tea. Slowly, her hands trembling, she put the kettle on and sorted out some cups and saucers. When I thought she was calm enough to take in what I was saying, I told her that I was leaving town that evening and would not be coming back. That got through to her. She pushed her fingers through her hair and took off her apron, throwing it over the back of a chair. She liked the idea that I was leaving so much that she even glanced into a mirror that hung on the wall, and pulled at the collar of her dress. I hoped she wasn't comparing it with my Paris rigout, but I'm afraid that she was.

'That's very sensible of you,' she said, regaining poise with every minute that passed. I suppose the pills were beginning to work, too. 'There's no place for you here. You've got your own friends in America, and I expect Pat left you well provided for . . . Americans carry lots of insurance, don't they?'

'I've money enough and friends of a sort, though not of the kind you can rely on through hard times. Life's not the same over there It's materialistic, self-centred and hasty. I liked it well enough when Pat was alive, but ours was an unusual marriage because we never knew when Pat would get ill again; because of that we tried to make everything we did perfect for the other. I never kidded myself that it would be the same without him, and it isn't. I'm tired, Mary. I dreamed of coming back here and settling down somewhere close to you . . . but it's been brought home to me today that day-dreams have no place in the modern world.'

'That's right. You don't belong here.' Her behaviour was almost normal, now.

'About Johnny,' I said. 'I accept that he doesn't want to meet me yet, and I have to trust you not to turn him against me for good. There's his father to be considered, too. Have you told Johnny yet about his father?'

'No, I've decided it would not be right for him to know. He'll be going off to university in less than a month. I don't want his mind filled with nonsense about rich relations when it ought to be on his books.'

'And who is to pay? You want me to increase the allowance?'

'He got a scholarship, and as for the rest, we will manage.'

'But, Mary, there's no need for you to manage. I have plenty of money and—here ...' I took out the building society book which Edward had given me, and laid it on the table. 'This money has been laid by for Johnny by his father. Con will give you a cheque for the total in a few days' time.'

'Johnny doesn't need the money. He's not like you, a parasite living on other people's earnings. We've brought him up to fend for himself.' Nevertheless, she picked up the book and fingered it. No doubt she was thinking that her husband could do with the money, if Johnny didn't need it.

'Take it,' I coaxed. 'And of course I will continue Johnny's allowance. Whether you like it or not, both his mother and his father have money, and he'll be a rich man when we pass on. Suppose I asked Edward to arrange for Tom to be loaned some money, just to tide him over ....?'

She didn't like the idea. Her hand jerked as she made the tea, spilling boiling water on the table. She mopped it up with her apron.

'We don't want your money,' she said. 'We'll manage.'

'Would you like to adopt Johnny?'

'What do you mean? He is ours already.'

'Not legally. Suppose I were to arrange it —I think Edward would agree—then Johnny would bear your name legally. All I ask is that we are allowed access, his father and I. Edward must be allowed to meet the boy when he wishes, and you must send him to see me in New York for a couple of days every year. Surely that would satisfy everyone?'

She worked it out. If I were leaving, she had nothing to fear from me, and as for Edward, he had not contacted her before, and he might never get around to doing so.

'You must think I'm a fool!' she said, 'Bribing me to sell Johnny. You make me laugh! To think I've made myself ill, worrying about what you might do! Johnny is mine, and I'm keeping him! Take your money, and take Mr Hypocrite Straker's money, and get back where you came from!'

I had hardly touched my tea, but I stood up and backed away, so powerful was her fury.

'I shall have my solicitors write to Johnny direct,' I warned her.

She threw the teapot at me. It smashed against the wall. I fled, sucking my hand where it had been scalded. In the hall I brushed past some coats on a hat-stand which had once stood in the hall of the house where I had been born and brought up. One of the coats would be Johnny's. So near and yet so far away.

Jack was with the brown-haired girl in the garden next door, talking. He waved to me, and disappeared indoors with her. I collapsed into his car, wondering if there was anything I could have said to Mary to make her change her mind. Perhaps it wasn't surprising that I had failed to get through to her; she was so much older than I, she had been married straight from school, and had never known what it was to earn her own living. She had always behaved more like a disapproving aunt than an elder sister, and when I became pregnant she had treated me as if I were a naughty little girl who could be scolded into good behaviour. Come to think of it, yesterday was the first time we had met as adults.

My throat ached, and I wanted to cry, but felt it would not be fair to land Jack with a crying female twice in one day. I wanted Pat, badly. I'd been floating along on a make-believe dream of the future, of the day when I would return home to queen it over all those who had despised me before, and live in a Never Never Home with Edward and Johnny, Happily Ever After.

But real life wasn't like that. Real life had to take other people's wishes into consideration, and then the wishes of the people who were dependent on them. . . .

I was in pain, but I wasn't sure whether it was Edward or Pat whom I wanted most.

Another quarter of an hour passed and Jack came out, waving goodbye.

'Nice cup of tea,' he said. 'Tennis tournament next. Priory Gardens.'

He hadn't been wasting his time, for he

had learned where Johnny was to be that afternoon, and proposed to follow him there. He said that Hazel Meredith and her much younger sister Sally had lived next door to the Blakes for the last ten years. Hazel taught at a local primary school, and was Mary's closest friend. Hazel was a fine girl, Jack reported, who had been puttting up with a bloke who wasn't sure whether he would marry her or not for years. This bloke's mother didn't like Hazel, or something, and although they'd got engaged, they'd never got married. 'And not likely to now, either,' said Jack, with satisfaction.

Fast work! I thought, and suppressed a pang of jealousy for Hazel. I didn't want Jack, and if my return had jolted him out of his depression into looking around for someone else, then I must rejoice for him. Hazel Meredith sounded suitable, if a little dull. I would have thought Marge Lawrence more in his line—and smaller than him, too—but he had pronounced himself uninterested in Marge and was finding it difficult to take his mind off Hazel.

'Johnny is partnering young Sally Meredith in the Finals, Junior Section,' said Jack as we drew up at the Priory grounds. 'Due to start any minute, if they haven't started already.' He squeezed my elbow. 'They're unofficially engaged, I'm afraid.'

'Hazel and . . .?'

'Johnny and Sally. She is one year older

than him, but she's been mad about Johnny for years. Hazel says he's never been out with anyone but Sally, although that might be laziness on his part, what with her being next door and playing tennis together and so on. The Blakes are very keen on the idea of their getting married as soon as he's through university. He's going to be some kind of engineer.'

It had never occurred to me that Johnny would have found himself a girl already. I couldn't think why, for I'd been younger than him when I'd fallen for Edward.

Jack steered me into the club grounds and found a couple of seats for us. There were three tiers of benches around the main court, and we were on the topmost tier. There were people playing on the court, but at first I was too confused to distinguish between them.

'Far side,' said Jack, *sotto voce*.

Then I saw him. Nothing in the black and white photographs which Mary had sent me had prepared me for the fact that my son's hair was so outrageously red. It wasn't auburn like mine, nor was it the bright corn colour that Edward's had been; it was a true carroty-red, an exuberant mop which bounced around his ears and over his forehead as he leaped about the court. He was tall and well-set for his age, and in repose he was good-looking though not outstandingly handsome. He resembled me rather than his father, but in his mobility of expression he was like Jack, and because his features were rarely still, he did not give the impression of being a teenager. He looked older than he was. His personality was strong; he dominated the court. Now and then he laughed when he or his partner played a good stroke.

I was bewildered, because his photographs had prepared me so little for the reality of him. I was so happy I thought I might well explode in tears.

It was some time before I could take my eyes off Johnny to examine his partner. She was recognisably kin to Hazel Meredith but much smaller, and her long brown hair was tied back in a pony-tail. A serious, over-thin slip of a girl, she was not pretty, but she had an excellent forehand. Johnny covered her backhand with ease, demonstrating the hours of practice they had done together. I wondered if they also spent hours in bed together, and thought it likely. I was conscious of tearing jealousy, far worse than I'd felt when Jack announced his interest in Hazel.

'They ought to win,' opined Jack. 'They make a good pair.'

All right, they did. I fought jealousy, telling myself I was being ridiculous, hating a girl I'd never met because she spent more time in my son's company than I ever would.

They won the first set and changed ends. Passing the umpire's chair, Johnny threw his racket in the air, spinning it, and as it came down he saw me. He let the racket drop.

He knew who I was. He had Edward's eyes.

Sally spoke to him. He didn't hear her. I saw him take a deep breath and transfer his attention from me to Jack. I saw him wonder if Jack was his father, but I couldn't be sure whether he approved of us or not. I thought that, on the whole, he didn't.

The umpire turned in his seat to enquire the reason for the delay. Johnny walked to his place. It was his turn to serve; he served a double fault. And again. Sally spoke to him, her face hard. I started to pray. I thought: she's wrong for him—small-minded—too self-willed. He served an ace. He played brilliantly after that, but he didn't look at us again, and when the match was over and it was announced that he and Sally had won, he went off the court with her without a backward glance in our direction.

'Well!' said Jack. 'I wouldn't have missed that for worlds. A pity he doesn't want us to introduce ourselves. Too public here, perhaps! I can't help thinking I've seen the lad somewhere before, but where . . .? He's like you, isn't he? And yet not. When you know, you can see the likeness, but you wouldn't spot it, without prompting. You look as if you could do with another drink, Kit. Where can we get one at this time of day? I know. Come back to my house and see what I can find. You've

88

never seen my place, have you?'

He put his arm under mine and set me in motion. I got into his car, fastened my seat belt and tried to think while he chatted away about this and that. Jack would have made a very inefficient criminal, because his stream-of-consciousness speech gave him away, time and time again. He was talking about Sally now, and instead of considering the girl on her merits, was comparing her unfavourably to her elder sister.

I said, 'You do realise, Jack, that if you marry Hazel, and Johnny marries Sally, you will be brother-in-law to your own nephew?'

That stopped him. 'I hadn't got as far as that,' he protested, and blushed so painfully that he had to stop the car and pretend that the windscreen needed cleaning in order to cover his confusion.

'Have you arranged to see her again?' I asked.

'She wouldn't look at me,' he mumbled, getting back into the car. 'Widower, and all that. Not exactly good-looking, either.'

'Dear Jack, you know women have always fallen over themselves to make you notice them. I'm sure she's no exception. She strikes me as being a very genuine sort of girl, who wouldn't play around with you, but give you a straight yes or no. Why don't you ask her if she'd like to go with you to Piers' party tonight?'

'She'd never come . . . short notice like that! Only met her today . . . wouldn't have the nerve to ask her, anyway.'

We were near the city centre by now. I got out of the car and shut the door. 'Go and see her,' I said. 'I'll walk from here, or get a cab. Goodbye, Jack, and the best of luck. I don't suppose we shall meet again, but I'll always remember you.'

I walked back the way we'd come and turned into a side street knowing he couldn't follow me against the flow of traffic. I hoped very much that he'd find Hazel at home, and that she would listen to him. I rather thought she would.

*   *   *

Time was getting on, but I couldn't leave without having a final word with Tinker. I had forgotten that it wasn't that easy to come by a taxi in my home town; normally you phoned for one, or picked one up either from the station or Market Square. I had to walk the whole way to the garage, cursing the heat and my tight shoes and whoever it was who hated me enough to blow up the car I'd been using. I passed the Municipal Baths and wished I had time for a dip, even in that gloomy hangar. I loved water. On a day like this in the States I'd be beside or in the pool at one of the establishments Pat had left to me. In New

York I would have had an air-conditioned apartment and car . . .

Tinker was on the forecourt when I arrived. He was not pleased to see me. His son was in his office, and looked suspicious when he saw me arrive on foot. I could tell both men were thinking that I'd had an accident with their car. My arrival meant trouble all right.

I marched into the office, commandeered Tinker's chair, eased off my shoes and asked Tinker's son to fetch his father, please. It was bliss to sit down and cool off, but I couldn't help wishing Tinker had had a water-cooler installed.

It was five o'clock, nearly. I could make the six o'clock train, with luck.

'What's up?' asked Tinker, returning with his son. 'The car's all right, isn't it?'

'If only it were a simple matter of a puncture . . .!' I said. 'Tinker love, sit down, will you? And your son, too? I'm in trouble, and I need your help.' I told them everything that had happened to me since my arrival, omitting all mention of Johnny and his relationship to Edward, and confining my mention of the Slakes to talk of family discussions. I told them of the assault on me, and of the loss of my bracelet; at which Tinker looked startled and put his hand automatically on his desk. I learned later that the charm he had given me had been returned to him since our meeting that morning, and that he didn't particularly wish his son to learn of its existence. I didn't falter in my narrative, but went on briskly to describe the phone calls I had had, the people I had visited, and at last what had happened to the car they had rented me.

'We're insured, of course,' said Tinker. 'Although come to think of it, acts of terrorism may not be included in the policy . . .'

'That's not the point,' I said. 'The police don't yet know that I hired the car, and I don't intend to tell them unless I have to. If I do tell them, I won't be able to leave town tonight, because they will want to take statements from me and you and everyone else I have contacted since I arrived. I have been trying to make out a list of the people they may wish to question and it goes something like this: both the Strakers, Morton Ferguson at the bank, Fred Greenwood the estate agent, Con Birtwhistle and you two. Then there is my sister Mary and her husband Tom, Sheila Greenwood and her lover, Amy Straker and her son Piers, and to round off the list I suppose I must include Marge Lawrence the interior decorator.'

They gaped. This Was Life! they seemed to be thinking.

'Which of them done it?' asked the boy.

'I wish I knew.'

Tinker had gone into a slow burn. He reached for the phone and started to dial.

'That's my bloody car they've damaged,' he said. 'I'm phoning the police!'

FOUR

'Stop that!' Tinker's son killed the call. 'Use your common, Dad! Most of the people she's mentioned are good clients of ours and they won't want the bogies around asking questions.'

He gave his old man the high sign, and I smiled to myself, wondering exactly what tax fiddle Tinker was running that he should prefer to keep the police at arm's length.

'What I thought was,' I said, 'that I could write you out a cheque to cover the value of the car, and that if you are put to any expense in recovering it, then I will reimburse you. I am leaving town tonight and I won't be returning. I shall say nothing to the police about having been connected with the car in any way. In due course I suppose they may ask, as a matter of routine, whether you had hired this car out. You will act surprised, say yes you did and were wondering why the American lady had failed to return it at the end of her week's rental. They will then contact me in New York, and I will say that yes, I did hire it, but had to return to New York earlier than I expected and simply had forgotten all about the car and wasn't that terrible of me! Here's my address in New York; you can contact me, reversing the charges, if anything goes wrong.'

Tinker took my card, and frowned over it. 'The police have a right to know,' he said.

'What good would it do?' I asked. 'I have an enemy in town but to discover who it is would mean raking up the past, old flirtations, old jealousies, causing trouble unnecessarily. When I go, the trouble will go with me, and none of my old friends will be hurt. Why should you, or anyone else, be investigated by the police for the sake of a few hours' flirtation nineteen years ago?' I stifled the memory of Tinker happily having it off with me night after night in the long grass down by the river. And me enjoying it. Skilful little brute, he'd been. I hoped his wife appreciated him.

Tinker gave in. 'Well, if you put it like that . . .!'

'The police suspect it may have been an IRA bomb. Let them go on thinking that.'

'While the real villain gets away with it? It couldn't have been the Strakers, either of them. It would never occur to them. Not Fred—the great soft baby! Not Morton— he'd be afraid he'd be found out and lose his pension! The Blakes? I don't know them. What does he do?'

'I can't really see him doing it,' said I, thinking of my big, slow-moving brother-in-law. Yet he hadn't been at home that afternoon, and he hadn't been watching Johnny play tennis. I supposed he was at work. It would be easy to check up. No, I didn't want to do any more prying into other people's lives. I would go, and everything would return to normal.

'A woman might have done it,' suggested Tinker's son. 'That Marge Lawrence has got the devil of a temper, I know, because I heard her in action when one of our lads accidentally splashed her with petrol . . .'

'I don't know, and I don't want to know,' I said wearily. I picked up my handbag, eased myself back into my shoes and tottered out into the forecourt. How the devil was I going to get back to the hotel? I couldn't rent yet another car from the Mayhews—or could I? A blue Mini cruised along the road before us. There was yet another blue Mini parked at the petrol pumps, having a refill. A young married woman was at the wheel, and there were two children in the back.

A Mini. Blue. Driven by a dark man whom I'd thought I had recognised. He had followed me around all morning and, yes, he had parked in the Market Square when I went into the hotel to meet Edward. I closed my eyes in order to concentrate. The telephone call warning me that my car was in danger . . . going to the window . . . looking out . . . the explosion . . . people running, screaming . . . Yes, the man in the blue Mini had been leaning against his car watching as mine burst into flames. He hadn't ducked, or run away, or shouted when the car went up.

Just now . . . had it been the same man? I thought so.

'Do you know a dark-haired man who drives a light blue Mini?' I asked the Mayhews. 'It's not a new car, but not very old, either. Yellow number plate. Some kind of mascot dangling by the driving mirror. The man is tallish but not heavy, with stylishly cut smooth dark hair. He's wearing a brown tweed jacket over a high-necked brown pullover, and black trousers. Pale face, long moustache. He's been following me around all morning and I think he may have had something to do with the explosion.'

'Mr Hinds!' they said, almost together.

'You know,' Tinker prompted my memory. 'The one they used to call "Slim Jim". The one you couldn't stand. He runs a blue Mini, though I'd have said it was more of a mid than a light blue. You think it might be him?' He sounded pleased.

Slim Jim Hinds. Yes, I remembered him now. He was Bet Hinds' cousin, but not nearly so nice, and he had been one of those who used to pester me in the old days. I remembered now that I'd had to slap his face in public once. Could he have held a grudge all these years?

'What does he do? Where might I find him? If I could have a talk with him before I leave it might help to straighten out the car business for you.'

The Mayhews looked at each other,

'He doesn't do much since the divorce,' said Tinker. 'He tried to touch all his relations for money, until even Con grew tired of him and Bet told him to go on the dole like everyone else who was out of a job. He got slung out of his father-in-law's firm, see, and had to take a job as a travelling salesman. I don't know why he lost that second job. The last I heard he was answering ads for just about anything. He even had the nerve to ask if I'd take him on as a car salesman, but I said I valued my reputation too highly. Don't know where you'd find him now.'

'Mrs Greenwood's place?' suggested his son.

'Ah, that's about it,' said Tinker. 'But not a word to Fred, mind! Dick'—this to his son—'take Mrs Neely out there, wait for her and then drive her back to the hotel when she's ready to leave. Use your head, now,'—to me—'leave Dick outside the house to time your visit. If you're not out in half an hour, he'll ring the police. Right?'

Dick had a low-slung sports car which he had hotted up, and I found the ride uncomfortable, if informative. Dick was the chatty type. Sheila Greenwood had taken the children and gone back home to Mum and Dad Ferguson, who lived in an enormous house on The Hill, miles away from my sister; all the best people were to be found on The Hill, because it was close to the golf

97

club. Sheila didn't have a job, but helped her parents and the au *pair* girl run the house, and looked after the children. Jim Hinds was not allowed to sleep there, of course, but he had made himself useful as an odd job man while he was out of work, and the Fergusons didn't actively object to his spending most of his free time in Sheila's company. The odds were two to one that we would find him there.

'She's got the whole of the upstairs for herself and the kids,' said Dick, as he drew up outside a big, nineteen-twenties house. 'Her Hillman needs a lot of attention, and I've been out here several times to attend to it when she couldn't get it to start. It's in the garage, I see, so she's here all right, but it looks as if she's got a visitor.' A Bentley stood in the drive. 'Yes, it's Lady Muck all right.'

'Who?' The garage was empty except for the Hillman, so neither Jim nor the Fergusons were there.

'Mrs Paul Barnes. The wife of one of our Members of Parliament. I shouldn't take the mickey, really! She's one of the best women drivers I've come across.' He got out jerkily, and opened the bonnet of the car, saying he'd give me half an hour.

I went up the drive because that was what I had come to do, but I didn't have much enthusiasm for a talk with Sheila—especially with Joan Barnes listening in. The idea that Jim and Sheila might have combined to

98

persecute me because of grudges that were now nineteen years old, appealed less and less.

And yet Sheila had cried that morning and Con seemed to think that I was at least partly to blame for her tears. If my presence had been hurting Fred's chances of getting Sheila back, then perhaps I ought to see her, if only to assure her that I really was going.

A slim teenager opened the door, biting at an apple.

'Mum, it's for you!' she yelled, and from the depths of the house came the sound of heavy shoes descending an uncarpeted staircase. The teenager disappeared, leaving the door open. I stepped inside.

I wouldn't have recognised Sheila if I hadn't been expecting to see her. She towered over me in a bright red jumper and modish grey slacks. She knew who I was all right. She had a pale skin and fine eyes; both began to register anger that I had dared to approach her in her sanctuary. The interview seemed likely to be as disastrous as had been the one with Mary.

Before she could order me off the premises, Joan Barnes made an entrance down the stairs after her. Joan never walked into a room, but always Made an Entrance. She was the sort of person who could make a funny story out of the butcher's having given her the wrong joint, and a drama out of a flat tyre.

'Darling!' she cried and, making a swooping pass at my left cheek with hers, she pressed her fingers around my shoulders and gave me a shake of welcome. She was acting the part of Hostess, but her gesture of friendship was meant to be taken at surface value.

'Darling!' she said again, feeling for a handkerchief. 'Dammit, I am going to cry, and it always disturbs my contact lenses! Someone said you were only on a flying visit, but I said I didn't believe it because you wouldn't leave without coming to see me.'

'Dear Joan!' I said. 'Thank you. I wish I could, but I'm leaving again tonight.'

'Why don't you telephone me tomorrow . . . bother this party tonight, or you could come back with me now for a good chat! Ring me, and we'll arrange to meet somehow, either in London or New York. I was over in New York with Paul last year, but didn't have your address.' She put two fingers in her mouth, blew a porter's whistle, and collected a handbag from a table nearby. Footsteps thundered down the stairs and a long-legged pair of boys raced an even longer-legged girl through the hall, and out of the front door.

'Animals!' remarked Joan. 'Have you any children, Kit? However, they have to be fed and I have to change and find Paul's cuff-links, so I'll be off.' She turned in the doorway to add, 'Now behave, both of you!'

She slammed the door behind her, and the house felt cold. No central heating on at this time of year, of course. Not in good old, chilly

100

old England.

'Would you like a drink?' Sheila was making a big effort to be polite.

I had only had a couple of sandwiches for lunch, and a sip of tea since. I couldn't face the thought of drink. 'Might I have a cup of coffee, or tea?'

She looked incredulous, but led the way upstairs to her own kitchen. Her kitchen was an improvement on Mary's as far as equipment was concerned, but the atmosphere was just as icy. She asked if I'd like to wait in her sitting-room. I said I would rather talk to her, if I might.

'News travels fast,' I said. 'How did Joan know I was leaving?'

'Paul had lunch with Fred, who said you were running around telling some mad story about having been attacked. He told Joan, and Joan told me. If you came back solely to make trouble . . .'

'But Fred didn't know that I was leaving again so soon.'

'Oh, Bet told me that. She rang after lunch to see if I wanted a lift to the party tonight. I told Joan when she came to collect her brood. We have a working arrangement to have each other's children one afternoon a week in the holidays. They play tennis and swim and go to the pictures *en bloc*.'

She slapped a cup of coffee on the table and pushed the sugar basin at me. I tried to analyse her attitude and came to the conclusion that now her initial impulse to anger had been dissipated by Joan, Sheila felt no more than an impersonal dislike for me. She was not projecting the hatred I would have expected to feel from someone who had attacked and persecuted me.

'I didn't see you at the hotel last night,' I said, prolonging the conversation because I wanted time to drink my coffee.

'I was there all right. I saw you. Fred tried to stage another of his scenes, so I left. Luckily I'd taken my own car, or I might have had to sit there and listen to him.'

'Wasn't Jim with you?'

'Now who's been talking? I was on my own. If you must know, and I suppose the news will be all over town soon, he's left town. He got himself a good job in Manchester and gave up his room last week. I don't expect to see a lot of him in the future.'

'I thought I saw him today, driving around in a blue Mini.'

'He sold his car last week, when he heard he was going. He gets a car with his new job, and he needed the cash to set himself up in a flat in Manchester. He sold the Mini to a friend of his—Bates, or some name like it. Cates? Bates, I think. I expect it was him you saw.'

So out went Jim. Whoever it was who had followed me around, it hadn't been Jim. She started to peel potatoes, throwing a glance out of the window now and then; her children were playing in the garden below. I decided that, like me, she was basically the maternal type who needed someone to look after. She didn't make the best of herself, though. She wore next to no make-up, her hair was a mess, and the scarlet of her sweater didn't suit her style.

'Why did you come to see me?'

'Because of Fred. I don't wish him any harm, and I don't like to think what the police will have to say to him. Someone has been trying to kill me. I was attacked last night, just after I saw Fred at the hotel. My bracelet was taken . . . the charm bracelet I always wore, you remember? Fred's going around saying that he got his charm back through the letterbox this morning, but suppose he didn't? Suppose it was he who attacked me? He had the opportunity and the means, and he was the only one of my old friends who didn't welcome me back with open arms. He's made it quite clear to me that he thinks I'm a threat to his hopes of being reconciled to you . . .'

'What absolute nonsense!' she cried. She was getting angry again.

I knew it was nonsense, but it didn't suit my plan to admit it. 'I'm going to leave town tonight, but I'm going to ask the police to investigate Fred's movements. Be sure that they will. Attempted murder and robbery with violence, accompanied by threats to kill me if I don't leave town tonight . . . what

103

do you think he'll get for it? I don't see why you're getting so cross! Isn't this going to be marvellous ammunition for you when it comes to a divorce? You'll be able to get whatever you ask for in the way of alimony, and bar him from access to the children!'

'You are crazy! He wouldn't do a thing like that! What harm has he ever done to you . . .?'

I picked up my handbag and went out on to the landing, where I had seen a telephone.

'What's Fred's number?' I asked her.

She was actually wringing her hands She told me. I dialled. 'It's either this or ring the police; we'll get him over here and talk to him. He won't confess to me, but he might talk to you.' The telephonist at the estate agency put me through to Fred. 'Fred, I'm at the Fergusons' house, talking to Sheila. You'd better get over here, quick!'

Fred's voice quacked alarm.

'At the double!' I said. 'All hell's let loose here, and only you can sort it out.'

I replaced the receiver without waiting for his reply, and hauled my weeping hostess into what I guessed to be her bedroom. I was right.

'What are you doing? Let go of me!'

'Haven't you anything soft and frilly to wear? Not black or white, but something in a pastel shade . . .?' I found a pretty housecoat which looked as if it had been a Christmas present. She went on objecting through her tears. while I got her changed, brushed her

104

hair into a prettier style, and picked out a pretty lipstick for her to wear.

'That's more like it,' I said, as she actually made a move to help herself by blotting her lips. 'You're not the type to let your man get away just because he made eyes at an *au pair* girl, are you? You've taught him a lesson he'll never forget and now you're prepared to take him back because he's threatened by the police ... You don't believe he's a villain, do you?'

'He isn't!' she said. Her tears had stopped. Sheila's timing was appallingly bad.

'Try to keep the tears flowing,' I begged her. 'He'll be here in a moment ...'

I disposed her in an armchair in her sitting-room, lowered the blinds so that the early evening sun did not make her squint, and ran. I was right on my deadline, and I didn't want Dick Mayhew phoning the police. He was revving up the engine as I tore out of the house. I waved to him and cried that he should hold on just one more second, for I had seen another car speeding up the road, and I hoped it might be Fred. Luckily, it was.

'What's the matter?' he gasped. 'Is Sheila all right? There hasn't been an accident or anything, has there?'

'Idiot!' I told him. 'Go straight up, into the sitting-room, and give her a big hug. I gave her a scare to make her realise she didn't really want to let you go. Jim's gone, and she's all alone. Don't argue with her, don't attempt

105

explanations . . . just be a bit physical.'

'What?'

I stepped into Dick's car, waved goodbye and eased off my shoes.

'No go?' asked Dick.

'It wasn't Jim. Sheila knows nothing and cares less. I'm sorry to have dragged you all the way over here on a fool's errand.'

'My pleasure.' He sat straight, preening himself. I was amused to see that he was every bit as randy as his father had been, and that he was about to make a pass at me.

'It's a pity you're going,' he said. 'Why not put it off till tomorrow, and let me show you the sights of the town tonight? I'm supposed to be going to this stuffy party with Dad, but there'll be so many people there they'll never miss me. How about it?'

'That's the nicest offer I've had for months. It takes years off my age! Thanks, Dick, but I really must catch that train. You go off to the party and drink a glass of wine to me; I'll have supper on the train and return the compliment.'

He was satisfied with that. We drove into the Square. I was thankful to see that the wreck of my car had been towed away. Dick helped me out of the car and went with me to the hotel steps, to make sure I would be safe, as he put it. I shook hands with him and went inside, checking my watch. I didn't think I'd make the next train. Perhaps I could have a sandwich in the bar while I killed time for the one after it.

'Letter for you, Mrs Neely,' said the receptionist. 'And a couple of phone calls. Also your bill, and we've got you a reservation for tonight at the Dorchester.'

I paid my bill and went upstairs to finish my packing. Nothing had turned out as I had planned; I felt old and depressed. One of the phone messages was from Edward, but he hadn't said anything about calling back. So that was that. By tomorrow I would be well out of his reach.

I must not cry.

The other phone message was from Jack, saying that he had taken my advice and been successful beyond his expectations. Dear Jack —I was delighted that he should have a second chance.

The last envelope contained an expensive, embossed invitation from Mr and Mrs Edward Straker for their party that night, to celebrate the eighteenth birthday of their son Piers at White Wings. R.S.V.P. Someone had written on the back, 'Do please come—my brother will call at the hotel to collect you!' It couldn't be genuine!

Was someone having a joke at my expense? I tore the card across and then put the pieces together again. Did I, or did I not recognise the handwriting?

The phone rang. The receptionist

announced that Mr James Coulster had arrived, and was waiting for me in the bar. Amy's brother, the one who hadn't wanted to go into the works, thus creating a vacancy which Edward had been elected to fill.

I couldn't understand what was going on. If Amy had sent me the invitation . . . But why?

I tore down the stairs. There were quite a few people in the bar, but I would have picked James out any time. He was as tall and as slim as Amy, his hair as curly, his face even longer and narrower. His eyes were restless and his forehead heavily lined. He looked as if he found life boring and as if he judged every man in terms of how much they were worth financially. I had seen him around once or twice in the old days, but he had never mixed with our set and never before acknowledged my existence. I seemed to remember that he spent most of his time sailing.

He recognised me. His eyes added up the cost of my lizard-skin shoes and matching handbag, Paris rigout, my engagement ring and emerald ear-rings. His bow as he introduced himself and ushered me to a seat indicated that he accorded me respect as a moneyed woman. I would never be his equal, because I had not been born to the purple, but I was worth a minimum of courtesy.

He switched on the charm. So sorry we'd never met before, better late than never, glad to have the opportunity before I left town again, and so on. Hoped I'd got the invitation from Amy, sorry about the short notice, hoped I'd spare the time to pop in on the party . . .

'Yes, but . . .!' I said.

'Amy said I must be sure to get you there early.' He looked at his watch. 'My father, the Alderman, is to show you around. He couldn't fetch you himself because he doesn't drive at the moment. Heart condition, you know. Time for one small drink. What would you like?'

'Mr Coulster, I have a train to catch . . .'

'Don't worry about that. Have your drink, change, we'll take your luggage with us, you spend a little time at the party and then we'll get you to the station in time to catch the ten o'clock train.'

'This is crazy! Why should you want me at your party?'

'Edward and Amy seem to think it would be a good idea if you dropped in for a little while—kill the scandal, and all that.' He lifted a finger at the barman, who produced a brandy and ginger for me. I needed the drink. I didn't like to think of Edward and Amy discussing me behind my back.

'Amy thought it would be best to show everybody that there was nothing in these stories that have been circulating today. Upset everybody properly, haven't you? Jack and Fred and poor old Con and, of course, Edward. Amy said if you came to White Wings for an hour, and father showed you round as if you were an ordinary friend on a visit, and that you then went off to London in our car, the gossip would die down.'

'But the gossip will die down as soon as I've gone, anyway.'

'I don't know anything about that. All I know is that Edward and Amy asked me to pick you up and explain the situation to you. If you'll drink up and change, I'll get the porter to bring down your bags, and we'll be off. I want to be back at White Wings before the rush.'

'Edward is back with Amy? Is that what you are trying to say?'

'Yes. I paid his bill and collected his baggage from the Dragon this afternoon. I don't know what story he's been telling you, but this isn't the first time he's had a tiff with my sister and gone off for a couple of days.'

I tried not to cry. I stared at my reflection in the mirror behind the bar and willed myself not to cry. I would not show him how much I'd been hurt. Then anger came, and it seemed to me that it would be an admirable thing to go to this party and show them all that I didn't care.

James was looking at his watch.

'Can you be ready in five minutes?'

'I don't know. I'd like to come in some ways, but I promised Con I'd leave without causing any more trouble. Suppose I phone him, and ask his advice?'

'I shouldn't bother. He'll be on his way

there by now. You can see him at the party and explain. You'll be under our protection for the evening. We'll take care of you.'

'I don't doubt it, but . . .' I didn't really want to risk seeing Edward again, for my own sake. Knowing that he'd not even waited for me to leave town before he returned to his wife had left a sour taste in my mouth.

'Amy told me to tell you that she had come across something of yours that she would like to return to you. Something you lost last night, she said. Please, do come!'

Click. I knew who had attacked me last night and why they had taken the coat from the hotel.

Click. I knew why there had been no reply when I phoned White Wings later that evening.

Click. I knew who had intercepted my letter telling Edward I was pregnant, years ago.

I don't think I've ever been so angry in all my life.

'Give me ten minutes, and I'll be ready.'

*   *   *

I consider myself something of a connoisseur on parties and houses, having sampled the most luxurious entertainments the States can offer in the way of hospitality, and owning three beautiful houses of my own which had all, at one time or another, been featured in magazines devoted to interior decoration. Yet in all my years of party-going, I had to acknowledge that the party the Strakers threw at White Wings that night took an Oscar. The fine weather helped, of course; it was a beautiful evening and still warm enough at nine o'clock to stroll around without wondering where you'd left your coat. There was no wind, which meant that the fairy lights strung in the trees all around the lake and clustering over the rose garden were reflected in the waters. The setting was perfect; a bowl of trees declining to a natural lake, framing the white house and floodlit lawns.

If one were to search for a fault, it might be in the design of the house itself, which was of a period not much to my taste. It had been built, the Alderman told me, on the site of a much earlier house by a distinguished architect of the nineteen-twenties, and to my mind it suggested a ship, rather than a home. It was a two-storied affair, painted white, with single-storey extensions set in an arc to enclose a terrace which was paved with multi-coloured slabs. The principal bedrooms and the reception-rooms looked out over the terrace, down the smooth lawns to the lake, and you could drift into the long sitting-room from the terrace by the ranks of french windows.

If the weather had turned inclement, the Alderman said, there had been plans to erect a marquee on the terrace, but since this had proved unnecessary, a simple striped awning had been hung over it to provide a focal point for the party. Two bands, or rather one conventional dance band and one rock group, played alternately on the terrace, where couples danced, Drinks and a good-looking buffet were being dispensed from stalls which were set on the lawn in rows to resemble an old-fashioned market place; cold meats here, fish next to it, soup further on, etc. Log tables and benches were grouped under the ancient cedars for those who wished to sit and eat in civilised fashion.

The swimming pool was also floodlit, and in the changing-rooms beyond there were shelves of swim-wear and towels, waiting to be borrowed by the energetic. A hot-dog stall drew a crowd beside the pool, and beyond it there were tennis courts—now empty— vegetable gardens and greenhouses. A path led round the edge of the lake, and guests sauntered along it, whispering, giggling, playing hide and seek in a fairy-tale wood strung with lanterns. The brilliant clothes of the guests contributed to the beauty of the scene; even I, in my outrageously expensive lace, was only one bright star among many. On the lake a flotilla of brightly painted punts and row-boats, each equipped with its own lantern, scattered laughter and drops of water on each other. Down by the boat-house a lifeguard paraded, in front of the barbecue. White-hatted chefs carved enormous joints, sucking-pigs turned on spits, there were rumours that a famous rock star would perform . . .

'The fireworks are scheduled for a quarter-past twelve,' said the Alderman, 'after the cabaret, or whatever they call it nowadays. Yowling and howling, if you ask me, but that's what Piers wants. Everyone should be gathered over on the house side of the lake by that time. We ask everyone to douse the lights on the lake at midnight. The fireworks have been set up on the opposite side, so that we will get a good reflection in the lake. Edward and Amy have been months planning this party.'

'I can imagine. Isn't it time I was leaving?'

'I'll get you a drink first. Not on the terrace, it's too crowded. Come this way.'

There must have been five hundred people in the grounds already, but more were still arriving. The reception line was outside the front door, below the gardener's cottage. James Coulster had avoided the front door, and taken me into the house the back way, so that I had not yet had a chance to meet either my host or hostess. I hadn't complained, because as soon as I'd arrived I knew I didn't really want to see Edward again. The Alderman had been waiting to greet me, and had taken me over the house and grounds, talking in such a courteous fashion that I was unable to disentangle myself.

A man of sixty or so, with compressed

lips over a decided chin, he held my arm throughout, even when we met people I knew. So I had merely exchanged a couple of words with a surprised Con, and nodded at Jack. I was pleased to see that he had his brown-haired Hazel on his arm, and that neither of them cared that she topped him by a good inch. I saw Morton and nodded at him; Paul and Joan . . . I identified Piers by his likeness to his father; he was dancing on the terrace and too busy to stop to talk to us.

'This is Amy's sanctum.' The Alderman showed me down a short passage at the back of the house into a dark little room fitted out as an office. A tray of drinks was set on the desk, together with a plate of tiny sandwiches. 'What would you like? Amy will be popping in here soon to say hello. She said you might like a drink and a bite to eat before you went off.'

'Brandy, please. I am looking forward to having a chat with Amy; especially as I think she has appropriated something of mine.'

'As you had appropriated something of hers.' His tone was so gentle that I wondered if I had understood him correctly. He nodded, handing me my drink. 'The Coulsters know how to hold on to their own.'

'As you did when Edward tried to break free of Amy before they were married?'

'Just so. We had a considerable financial investment in that young man, which he has repaid, as was only right. Apart from his

115

fixation about you, he has justified Amy's decision to marry him. The dividends from the Mills have never been so high. A great pity that he has to go—we shall find it extremely difficult to replace him.'

'Surely, the question doesn't arise?' I gulped down the brandy and took a couple of sandwiches, to take the taste away. The Coulsters may have spent a small fortune on their party, but their brandy was not good. 'I'm leaving, and according to your son, Edward has already returned to Amy.'

'Another drink, while we're waiting for Amy?'

'Could you open a window? It's very hot in here.' My head felt strange . . . suffused . . . the ceiling was becoming darker and wavering at the corners . . .

The Alderman's face peered at me, close to, frightening me. I heard my glass drop on to the floor, but when I groped for it, I lost my balance and had to clutch at a chair to prevent myself from falling.

'Doped!' I enunciated the word with care.

He caught me in his arms and helped me on to the chair.

'Why?' I asked. 'What harm have I done you?'

'Money, my dear. We can't possibly let Edward take all his money out of the family, apart from the insult to Amy.'

I screamed. At least, I tried to do so, but

116

the sound I made was more like something produced from a tin whistle than the throat of a fully-grown woman. The door opened and through a thickening mist I saw Amy enter, followed by a thin, dark man. The man who had followed me in his blue Mini earlier in the day.

'But . . . why?' I asked. 'I'm leaving tonight.'

'Too late,' she said. 'I told you to be out of town by ten, or you'd die, and that's just what's going to happen. You're going to die!'

FIVE

I had thought I would be quite safe at White Wings because so many people I knew would be there. In a crowd, at a party, surely nothing could happen to me.

But it was happening. I fought sleep, weaving in and out of consciousness. I was sitting in a chair with my wrists held by the two men, steadying me . . . I started awake, feeling frightened, but they were only binding something soft round my wrists, bandaging them. Then someone was at my feet on the floor, crossing my ankles. I tried to rise and discovered that my ankles would not part. I was pressed back on to my chair, my wrists placed behind me, crossed, and held there. I could hear someone panting . . . it was me.

My head drooped forward. I was going to fall forward on to the carpet . . . I was caught round the shoulders and held upright. I was grateful for that.

Something cold stung my face. I got my eyes open and blinked at Amy, who was standing before me holding a siphon of soda water. The two men had disappeared. Once more I tried to get up, but found I couldn't move. A pair of nylon stockings had been knotted together to make a rope which bound my shoulders to the chair.

'No bruises, no marks,' said Amy.

'But why? I sent Edward back to you. I told him I wouldn't have him. I was going to catch a train early this evening.'

She picked up my evening bag and opened it. She was wearing long gloves.

'Of course I know it was you who followed me from the hotel last night. You were wearing a dark dress, and you are the right height. You took the coat from the hotel to put over your shoulders and arms, which were bare; the coat covered up your jewels and helped camouflage you.'

'It was not so warm last night. I had forgotten my wrap, that's all.'

'But when you saw that the light was missing in the alley, and that you could use one of the pipes for a weapon, you couldn't pass up the chance of disposing of me, is that right?'

'I intended to frighten you, merely. At

that time I was angry with Edward, but it did not seem to me that the situation was irredeemable.' She picked out my powder compact, put it in her own handbag, and threw mine on my lap.

'It was you who took my bracelet. You returned the charms to their original owners, and to me, by way of reinforcing your threats, but you kept the bracelet itself, and the charm which Edward gave me. What have you done with them?'

She unlocked a drawer in her desk and withdrew the bracelet with the gold heart still clinging to it. She knelt down behind me, and I could feel her fingers busy at my wrist, fastening the bracelet above my bonds.

'I don't understand you,' I said, fighting sleep. 'You have a lover. Why don't you let Edward go? You don't love him.'

'I bought him. He is mine. He was nothing when I selected him. I made him what he is, and he has been a credit to me in some ways. No one else had precisely that combination of looks and ability which I was looking for. He was penniless, and I gave him everything he wanted. He has never been grateful enough. He has always set his will against mine, over Piers' upbringing, and altering the grounds here, though of course I would not let him touch the house; then filling the place at weekends with his motley collection of friends, and insisting on our inviting people who are a handicap to us socially, like that mechanic, Mayhew; squandering his time at that breeding-ground for criminals which he calls a Boys' Club; disappointing me over our projected tour of the West Indies solely because his sister-in-law had died and that snivelling brother of his made himself ill with grief; bringing that smelly dog into the house; he even had the nerve to oppose my wish to make Piers a director on his birthday . . .'

'You never loved him, then. You couldn't talk like that if you did. You tricked him, fooled him right from the start. You told him you were pregnant in order to get him to marry you when he wanted to break off the engagement . . .'

'I believed I was pregnant at the time. It was only after we were married that I discovered that I wasn't.'

'It was you, and not Edward's father who intercepted my letter, and it was you who sent me that cruel reply . . .'

'With the money. Don't forget the money! Yes, I admit I took the opportunity to get you out of the way. If you'd stayed in town, he might have been tempted to make you his mistress later on, and I wasn't going to stand for that. Even then, it was tough going, breaking him in. He used to go on about values, and different life styles, and want to live without servants in a smaller house . . . I told him that if he didn't know what was due to a Coulster, I did, and he'd have to maintain me in the style to which I was accustomed, or else . . . It was sheer bad luck he discovered your letter. I knew I ought to have burned it, but I had had some idea it might come in handy one day, to use against him if he got too far out of hand. He was too valuable for us to lose by that time, of course, so we had to agree to his terms.'

'That's when he left you before! How long was that after I'd gone?'

'Piers was three. I had to send him down to the hotel to beg his father to come back in order to get Edward in a reasonable frame of mind. That cost us a packet, that little error of judgement—we had to give him a block of shares in the Mills and the freehold of this place. But I made sure he paid for it, over the years, and every time I've thought of your boy at the State school, and compared what he had to what my son had . . .'

'You knew that Johnny was still living here? And you didn't tell Edward?'

'Correct. I made it my business to find out everything I could about the Blakes and I've always kept my eye on the boy. It was I who arranged for him to meet the Ferguson boy last year, so that I could keep tabs on him, and it was I who arranged for him to be invited here tonight.'

She frightened me. 'Let me go. I have a train to catch.'

'I'm afraid that's not possible.' She took off one of my emerald ear-rings and dropped it in her handbag. 'You've caught your last train. In a moment or two Lewis will be back and you will be going on your last journey, down to the cellar. Do you know about our cellar? It was part of the house that originally stood here, years ago; it is very damp and sometimes it floods. It's ankle-deep in water already. The lake is fed by springs in the slopes around it, and one of the springs runs right under the cellar. Edward had the course of the spring diverted when we put in the sprinkler system for the garden, but it's very easy to send the water back under the house; all you have to do is turn a wheel on a valve set in the wall at the back of the house. Lewis understands these matters, luckily. I'm afraid, my dear, that you are going to get very wet.'

I tried to scream. She gagged me with another stocking.

'No marks,' she said. 'We're going to take you down to the cellar and tie you up so that the rising water will drown you. You mustn't drown too soon, or they may be able to trace the drug we used to subdue you. In a couple of hours, say. You will be drowned without a mark on your bodies. The cellar will probably fill to the ceiling, because the outlet has been blocked up, but don't worry about the house being damaged. At the right moment Lewis will turn the water back into the sprinkler

122

system and free the blocked drain so that we can recover your bodies. In the early hours of the morning, when everyone else has gone, we will take your bodies down to the lake and drop you in. An overturned punt nearby . . . a boating tragedy . . . so sad, such a terrible aftermath to such a marvellous party, but everyone will say it was probably a good thing, because it was obvious that you and Edward were running off together, and that would never do, would it? Yes, that's why I have taken your compact and your earring. I am going to leave them in Edward's bedroom, together with the wrap you wore on your arrival. I am going to disarrange the bed, make a mess in the bathroom, and altogether give the impression that you and Edward stole off to make love in his bedroom during the party, and afterwards ran away together, going across the lake because Edward had left his Rolls, with his luggage and yours in the boot, on the far side of the wood. There'll be a scandal, of course, but it will be hushed up for the sake of the grieving widow—that's me! The time, the place, everything is right. Edward was talking today of making a new will in your bastard's favour; well, I've put a stop to that, too. He may not have much voting stock, but he's acquired a large number of ordinary shares over a period of years, and I don't see why they should go out of the family. Edward and I made wills in each other's favour when we got married, and if he dies tonight, all his money, this house and his shares will return to the Coulsters, where they belong.'

I tried to cry out, but only made a mewing noise.

'Neither James nor my father will help you, needless to say. When danger threatens, the Coulsters stick together. I only had to go to Father last night and tell him that Edward wanted to leave me, for him to offer his aid. As for Lewis, I do not intend to marry him when I am free; he is well enough on his way, but no substitute for Edward as a business man. Lewis will have the lease of a second shop bought for him, and be thankful. He's done well, hasn't he? He's been shadowing you all day, and you never knew. He handed over to my chauffeur this afternoon while you were at the tennis match, in order to help with our little arrangement in the cellar, but otherwise he's been at your shoulder for nearly twelve hours, poor boy. Not that we can rest when we have you safely down in the cellar, for there will be Johnny to bring down after you, and then Edward. I think we'll have Johnny found in a different part of the lake from you and Edward; no need for your names to be linked. Your sister will inherit your money to compensate her for the boy's loss. All my anxieties disposed of at one stroke! You must admit, it's an admirable scheme!'

The door opened and Lewis came in. She

held the door open while he released me from the chair and, throwing me over his shoulder, fireman style, he carried me out of the room. We were in a dark corridor. I tried to kick, but he held me tightly, and anyway there was no one around to see us. Through a door and down some steps we went. I was dumped on to another chair. I fell off, and flopped about on the floor.

'She'll bruise herself,' said Amy anxiously. She was locking the door which led into the corridor,

'Doesn't matter,' said Lewis. He had taken off his shoes, and was donning a pair of fishermen's boots. We were in a semi-basement room, a larder whose shelves were filled with jam-jars, tins and cleaning materials. The floor was of stone flags and in one corner there were some steps cut deeper into the earth, ending in another door. Amy went down these steps and drew back the bolts on the door; they were new bolts, and the door was of oak, a good two inches thick. She pressed a switch on the wall beside her, and a dim light showed me a cellar within.

Lewis picked me up, and cursed because he had dropped my handbag. Amy rescued it and stuffed it into his pocket. Gingerly negotiating the steps and low doorway, he descended into the cellar with me on his shoulder. Swirling waters covered the floor and lapped his ankles. The cellar was large and inadequately lit by one naked bulb dangling from a wire which could be hooked on to fitments at different parts of the ceiling. The roof was supported by brick pillars, and though the walls had been white-washed once, they were now dingy and the brickwork was showing through in many places. There was the usual assortment of rubbish that accumulates in the cellar of a big house over the generations; a hideous Victorian sideboard, a pair of wooden-framed bunks, a pile of planks which had probably been used for decorating at some time, empty wine racks, broken chairs; and the body of a large dog. Crisp, Edward's much-loved pet.

Lewis threw me face down on to the straw pallet of the bottom bunk. He put his knee in the small of my back, undid the bonds which held my wrists together behind me, and, twisting wire around each bandaged wrist, he secured me to the uprights of the bed. Then, tugging at my ankles, he pulled me flat and secured my bound feet to the foot of the bunk. I couldn't move. I tried, and the effort wore me out.

'Can't think why she isn't asleep!' said Lewis. He tossed my handbag onto the bunk at my side.

'Different people react differently to drugs,' said Amy, who was standing on the steps, well above the water. 'Come on, Lewis—two more to go yet, and that water's coming in too fast for my liking. Are you sure you can clear the outlet when we need to rescue their bodies?'

'Positive. But if it doesn't work, I have my frogman's outfit in the boot of the Mini, and I can dive in for them. It would take longer, but the result would be the same.'

'I don't want you catching cold. You know how susceptible you are.'

I turned my head to watch him wade out. The water swished around his waders, making progress slow. It was evil-looking, dark, surging water. Dirty. I was lying so that I had to watch it rise, gently submerging brick after brick in the wall beside my bunk.

I began to cry.

I dozed and woke, shivered, noted the new level of the water, and dozed again.

Suddenly I was wide awake. Someone was coming down the steps, treading heavily. I couldn't see . . . No! A head of bright hair swung over Lewis's shoulder. Johnny, fast asleep.

The water swirled around Lewis's calves. He dumped Johnny on a crazily tilting chair, and tied him sitting upright to one of the brick pillars. Johnny's head lay aslant the bright yellow of his shirt, his mouth open. They hadn't bothered to gag him, I suppose because he had succumbed to the drug more quickly than I. Or maybe they'd given him more of it.

'Two down and one to go,' said Lewis, speaking not to me but to Amy, who was waiting for him on the steps as before. 'But

Edward's going to be difficult. He hasn't drunk anything at all yet. You know how little he drinks at the best of times. Does he suspect, do you think? Could we get him down here by telling him about the dog?'

'Yes, that's a possibility. No, I don't think he suspects anything. Neither of these two went past the reception line, and as far as I know he is unaware of their presence here. Even if someone does tell him that the woman is here, we can rely on him not to make a scene at Piers' party. He thinks he's following her to New York next week, so why should he suspect anything?'

'The Ferguson boy. Will he make trouble when the boy is found dead?'

'No. I've already told him that his friend has disgraced himself and was told to leave. When the boy is found in the lake, they'll think he had one too many and fell in, that's all.'

'Your father is feeling all right now? He'll be able to last the course? It would cause comment if he had to go home now.'

'I can't spare him yet. He's sitting down in my study. Anyway, who would drive him home? I can't spare my chauffeur. No, he'll have to wait until later. He's had these attacks before . . .'

Lewis climbed the stairs and went out. The door slammed and was bolted.

They had left the light on. The sight of the water rising around Johnny's legs drove me frantic. I wrestled with my bonds until sweat ran down my cheeks, but I could not shift them. The effects of the drug seemed to have worn off. I couldn't decide whether I wanted Johnny to wake before the water drowned him or not. My bunk was not very high off the ground and the water was lapping at the base of my pallet before Johnny stirred.

He yawned, squeezed his eyelids, and dozed off again. I couldn't speak to warn him. I could only watch him and the water alternatively as it rose around and soaked my pallet. The water was round his knees. Loose pieces of furniture and planks of wood had begun to float on the surface of the water.

Johnny's eyes opened and he looked straight at me. He stared. He blinked. He absorbed the fact that I was tied up. He inspected our surroundings. He tried to speak, and then to smile. I saw him bunch his muscles in an attempt to rise. And fail.

'It's a nightmare!' he said.

I shook my head.

'If it's not a nightmare, then you're my mother.' I nodded. He swallowed hard, took a deep breath and inspected the cellar once more. 'Why?' he asked. 'For God's sake, why?' He knew I couldn't reply, but he was like Jack, who also found relief in communication. 'Likewise, who?' he went on. Then he burst out laughing. There was shock and horror in his laughter, but also an appreciation of the funny side of the situation which had not occurred to me. 'Here's a how-de-do!' said my son. 'And you not even able to give your son a blessing as he falls to the earth, dying! Sorry, bad taste, that! Sorry about this afternoon, too. I behaved badly, running away like that instead of staying to be introduced. I could lay the blame on Sally, but that wouldn't be fair—likewise, not true. Oh, she doesn't want me to have anything to do with you or my real father, and she might well have been rude to you if I'd told her who you were, but it wasn't worry about what she might say that made me run away. Nor was it worrying about Mum—sorry, my foster-mother. I'm afraid I've been brought up to call them Mum and Dad, and it's too late to change that now. I'd never remember.' He watched me intently as he spoke, his facial expression altering from moment to moment, as Jack's did. I began to like him, as well as love him. 'Forgive me if I get the names muddled?' He grinned, all charm. 'Well, it's true that Mum has been trying to get me to promise not to see you, and what with her having had flu so badly early this year and the change of life and that, Dad—that's my foster-father, of course—said he'd appreciate it if I held back for a while and not contact you, and of course I said I would. That was before you came. I only heard you were here, in this country, when I got back home last night, and, Brother! Was that some row! We had to get the old doc. back to calm her down, and . . . well, I ended up promising her I wouldn't try to contact you yet, but wait for Christmas, when I'd settled in at the university. I'd waited so long, another couple of months wouldn't matter . . .' He looked grimly at the wall in front of him.

'Mum and Dad think I don't care about being illegitimate and not knowing who my real father is. That's not true, of course. I thought I was their son until I was twelve. I knew I didn't take after either of them, but they told me I took after my grandfather, and I accepted that. I was very badly shocked when I was told. I knew all about you, of course; my pretty aunt who sent me money from America at birthdays and Christmas . . . there was even a photograph of you in the family album. I could accept you as my mother and even be proud of you because you'd done well for yourself afterwards, and the Reverend told me many little things about you which made me like you. But not to know who my father was—that was bad! Mum and Dad said you didn't know, or wouldn't tell. The Reverend said that of course you knew and that it had been a sort of Romeo and Juliet affair, and that you'd been parted by bad luck and the fact that the man was already engaged to be married. He wouldn't tell me any more, no matter how much I asked. I couldn't leave it like that. I wanted to know! But there was no way of finding out, and gradually I accepted that I would never know, or perhaps only learn who my father was when I was grown up and it didn't matter.

'Maybe it wouldn't have mattered so much if Dad hadn't been such a . . . I was going to say "such a failure", but he's not a failure as a person. He's good and kind and a bit dim. I've always been able to run rings around him mentally, and Mum,' he shrugged. 'She's a darling, but she's a terrible clinger. She doesn't even read a newspaper or listen to the news or . . . I was lonely. I had nightmares in which I searched for my father down long corridors. I began to look at people in the streets, wondering if this man, or that, might be my real father. I knew he was a native of this town, and that he'd been in the playboy crowd, and that was all I knew. I'd look at the photographs of business men in the local paper and think to myself how it would be if that one or the other were my father, and what I'd feel about him. I used to cut them out and keep them in an envelope on top of my wardrobe and look at their faces every night before I went to bed. I liked one man's face better than the others—I won't tell you who it was but I got an enlarged photo from the newspaper offices later on, and kept that for ages. I built up a fantasy in which I elected him as my father, and used to go to him for advice and a chat now and then. Daft, really. I grew out of all that, later on. I burned all the photos, including the one of Mr Barnes . . .' He blinked, and shook his head.

'Sorry, didn't mean to tell you. Must be whatever it was that they used to drug me with, making me feel . . . . Go ahead and laugh if you like, but our M.P. is a good sort and he wasn't a bad model to take. He tided me over a bad patch, anyway, until I met this other man. I'm sorry if this upsets you, but I don't really need to know my real father any more. When you turned up with him this afternoon I recognised him; I don't suppose he'd remember me, but I've seen him around at the club now and then. I mean, I'm sure he's a very pleasant person, and I've never heard anything bad about him, but face to face with him like that I knew I couldn't feel towards him as a son ought to feel towards his father . . . and that's why I ran away.'

He was silent, his eyes on the shifting water. If he'd been looking in my direction he couldn't have failed to see that I was trying to tell him he'd got it wrong, but he kept his eyes down. I could see by the movements of his shoulders that he was trying to rub through his bonds, but I knew they had bound him with bandages and wired his wrists together, and I didn't think he'd manage to free himself.

The water flooded over my pallet and I reared my head in horror.

'Steady!' said Johnny. 'Someone will come. Just keep your chin above water.'

133

The water was so cold. And dirty. I tried not to panic, but watched Johnny. He had failed in his efforts to release himself, and was now considering what he should do next. He started to call for help. His voice echoed in the cellar, but no one heard. I hadn't heard a single sound from outside the cellar since I'd been brought down, even though I guessed we must be almost immediately under the terrace on which a band was playing. I shook my head at him.

He got the message, and stopped. He grinned at me. He was a brave lad.

'Sorry, luv,' he said. 'What a way to end a party, eh? I wish . . . I wish I hadn't run away this afternoon. I'd like to have shaken him by the hand. I think you and I would have got on all right, too . . . don't you? I'm sorry about Mum and Dad—they'll be frantic . . . and Sally! But maybe that's all for the best, because I knew it wasn't going to work out, even if she didn't. *He* showed me that. I didn't go complaining to him, you understand, but . . . he encourages you to talk, and he listens, and though he never gives advice unless you actually ask straight out for it, somehow the very act of putting your case to him makes it clear what you ought to do. The first Wednesday in every month. He goes to the club to play chess with anyone who wants a game, and that's how it started. I run the chess section there now, but we still have a game when he comes down. We don't talk much. He isn't the interfering sort, but he's always there. I'm going into the Mills when I qualify. He's fixed a lot of the lads up with jobs, but he said he'd tell his personnel officer not to let me in the gates until I was qualified. He was going to advance me the money to go to university if I didn't get a scholarship; got it all worked out how much I'd need and how much interest I'd have to pay him. Then Mum told me you'd been sending an allowance for me all those years and she could divert that from the housekeeping if I wanted to go to university, rather than borrow from an outsider. But I don't think of him as an outsider. I've known him for five years now, and if I did elect him my substitute father, I didn't see there was any harm in it. I think . . . I know that he will grieve, too . . .!'

My suspicion that Edward and Johnny had somehow managed to get together had become a certainty. Frantically I made noises to show Johnny I had something important to tell him.

He laughed at first. 'Sorry, luv! Impossible to translate, and all that. Is it important?' I nodded. He thought about it. The waters whispered as they clung to my neck, and my muscles began to ache with the strain of holding my head above water. My dress floated on the water around me.

'About my father?' he asked. I nodded

and then shook my head. 'Yes and no? Well, like I said—he's all right. An architect, isn't he? Makes them all laugh. I suppose I can understand what you saw in him . . .' I shook my head. 'Not about him but he is my father, isn't he?' I shook my head again.

Johnny's expression was as transparent as Jack's. I saw incredulous hope fight with disbelief, then joy won, to be replaced with doubt. I nodded.

'Really?' he asked. 'It couldn't really be him, could it?' I nodded. He bowed his head and was silent. The water tickled my chin. It was high around Johnny's chest. He would see me die, and then die himself. He didn't speak again, or not to me, anyway. I thought I heard him whisper something about 'not wanting to die', but I couldn't be sure.

The door at the head of the steps opened and Edward stepped in, calling for Crisp, his dog.

Johnny shouted, 'Sir, down here! Help!'

'What . . .?' said Edward. He peered down at Johnny, but didn't recognise him. The light was much dimmer in the cellar than in the larder from which he had come. He started down the steps, leaving the door open behind him. It slammed shut and we heard the bolts shoot home.

Edward threw himself back up the steps and hammered on the door. 'No!' He tried the handle, but it did not move the door. There was an appalled silence in the cellar, except for the rustle of planks shifting in the water.

'Sir—my mother!'

Edward heard his son's voice, but didn't seem to understand. He was on his knees on the top step, with the palms of his hands flat against the door and his head drooping. With horror I realised that he, too, had been doped and that he was about to sink into sleep. If he did, then I would die within the next few minutes, for the water was creeping over my chin.

'Sir! Father!'

Edward's head jerked up. He rubbed his eyes and looked around him. He made his way down the stairs slowly, leaning against the wall to keep himself upright. He was finding it difficult to focus on Johnny, and he had not as yet seen me. I didn't blame him. I was nearly submerged, and tiring fast.

'My mother—in the bottom bunk!'

Edward looked around, dazedly. 'Crisp?' he called. 'Where are you? Why are you hiding down here?' Then he saw me. He stared, apparently unable to move, or perhaps merely puzzled as to why I was in such a strange position.

'Cut her loose, or she'll drown!'

Edward set himself in motion. I remembered how hard I had found it to move my heavy body when I had first drunk my doped brandy, and I knew how he felt. He fumbled in his pocket and produced a pen-knife. He stumbled. Clutching at a plank which slipped from under his hand, he fell full length into the water. Water surged into my mouth. I tried not to swallow, to hold my breath, to force my aching back to hold the muscles of my neck steady . . . Edward emerged, his suit blackened and his fair hair slicked close to his head. He had lost his knife.

He didn't waste time groping for the knife, but reached me in one desperate lunge. He felt along my arms for my wrists. Great concentration was required of him to make any movement at all. He was fighting not only the water, but an almost overwhelming urge to lie down and sleep. He released my wrists, tore off my gag and helped me to kneel while he freed my ankles. Then he put my arms round his neck and lifted me on to the top bunk. As he did so, his head dropped to cradle in the angle of my neck and shoulder. He was muttering something about wanting to put me over his knee, and that I must promise never, ever to frighten him like that again . . .

'Never, darling! We'll sink or swim together from now on.'

'Very apt,' grinned my son, whose existence we had temporarily forgotten. 'Anyone for a dip?'

Edward was asleep in my arms. I shook him awake and told him to go and rescue his son.

'Who . . .?' he asked. 'Johnny's in America.

138

You said so.'

'No, darling, you only assumed that he was.'

'I'm here!' grinned Johnny. 'Come and get me. John Blake to you, Johnny Jeffries to my mother, and Lord knows what, legally. Come on! Or it will be a case of "Dead and never called me Father"!'

Edward was rocking on his feet, but he had managed to focus on Johnny. 'You are my son? But . . . I wondered, once or twice, but you talked so easily of your background. I thought it was wishful thinking on my part . . . but if I could have chosen, from the whole city . . .'

'Same here!' said Johnny.

They didn't grin at each other, or openly express delight, but Edward put his hand on his son's shoulder and firmed it before dipping underwater to free him. Planks, chairs and wine racks had broken loose and were floating on the surface of the water, hindering him. But at last Johnny was freed. Explanations were exchanged while we sat in a row on the top bunk to recover. Edward had to hear why I'd left Johnny behind, and what had happened to him as a result. He also had to hear the story of my adventures since my arrival, and what plans Amy had made for our disposal. Johnny related how he'd been invited to the party by the Ferguson boy, and knowing that it was in honour of Edward's son, had accepted out of curiosity to see the home and the son of

139

his patron. Within ten minutes of his arrival, Amy had asked him into her study for a chat; this had puzzled him, as he thought he'd been asked to the party because the Strakers were short of young men. However, being naturally polite, he had fallen in with Amy's invitation, accepted a drink and known no more till he woke up in the cellar.

Edward had gone back to the Mills for his meeting after he left me. He had been in a state of shock, hardly able to understand a word of what was being said around him. Then someone at the meeting had spoken of their seeing 'eye to eye', and Edward had recalled that I had not met his eye once while I'd been talking in the Square. He'd excused himself from the meeting and shut himself in his office until he thought he'd arrived at an explanation for my behaviour. A phone call to Con confirmed his guess. He'd drawn a blank when he tried to contact me at the hotel, but when the receptionist there told him I was checking out, he ordered his secretary to cancel his engagements for the following week and book him on the first available flight to New York. After that, he'd returned to White Wings to help with preparations for the party. When Amy told him I was leaving that day, he replied that he'd be following me—which had sealed his fate in Amy's eyes. He had not seen me arrive at the party, but Jack had told him I was there. On demanding an explanation from Amy, she had told him that I had been invited by her to stifle a scandal, and that she was relying on him not to make a scene and spoil things for Piers on his birthday. To which Edward had agreed. After a while he had received a message that the Alderman had been taken faint and would like to speak with him in Amy's study. He had gone in to him, and been pressed to take a drink. He found Amy's father tired, but content to wait until later to be taken home. Edward sought for the chauffeur, but he had disappeared—to take the Rolls round to the other side of the lake, in fact, although we did not know that at the time. Then the Alderman had told Edward that Crisp appeared to have eaten something which had disagreed with him, and that he was being sick in the cellar. Edward was furious, because he had left the dog with the gardener with strict instructions that he was not to be let back into the house on account of Amy's aversion to him. Edward had rushed down to the cellar. He had not seen anyone follow him, and did not know who had closed the door behind him. The result was the same, whether it was the Alderman, or Amy, or Lewis.

'So how do we get out?' demanded Johnny.

Our position, though uncomfortable, was not at that moment dangerous. The water continued to rise, and when Johnny dropped off the bunk, it washed around his thighs, but we could always retreat to the stairs, which

141

were brick-built and rose in a steep flight to the door.

'Unfortunately,' said Edward, 'This cellar lies half under the terrace and half under the sitting-room. The water level could rise to the ceiling in here, and still not flood through the larder and up into the house itself.'

'We'll be missed,' said Johnny.

'Amy has explanations ready for that contingency,' said Edward. 'In fact, if I were her, I wouldn't bother to retrieve our bodies at all. I would lay my trails leading away from this house, put a padlock on that door up there, turn the water back into the sprinkler system when it begins to flood the larder, and wait. Let time do her work for her. If we drown, all well and good. If we haven't drowned, we can be starved to death. No one will hear us down here. No one will search the house for us, because everyone will think we've gone. They may drag the lake for our bodies—they probably will; but there is an overflow beyond my property into the river, and they may think we've been swept along there. Either way, we're not expected to be in the house. If I were Amy, I would even go away for a while . . . a couple of months, maybe? She could leave Lewis or her chauffeur here in charge. Then at some convenient moment the bodies in the cellar could be retrieved and buried in the wood.'

'I don't think she'll do that,' I said, 'because

she needs to prove your death in order to inherit your money and shares in the Mills.'

'She's had that,' said Edward, grimly smiling. 'I altered my will this morning, leaving everything to you, or if you predecease him, to Johnny here.'

'I don't want it,' said Johnny horrified.

'Edward will teach you how to handle money,' I said. 'When we get out of here he's going to divorce Amy and make you legitimate, so you'd better start thinking of yourself as a moneyed man.'

Our first problem was to stop the water from rising any further, and since we were unable to send the waters of the spring back uphill, it made sense that we found and cleared the obstruction in the pipe which should have led the waters safely away from under the house in a drain leading to the lake. If Amy had caused a blockage in the drain, Edward explained, it was likely that she had somehow or other filled it in at its most accessible point, which was through an inspection hole covered by a grating in the floor of the cellar. The difficulty lay in locating this grating now that the floor was under a metre of water. The men took planks and started to scrape along the floor with them. Edward found the grating, took a deep breath and went underwater to try to ease it off. He failed. Johnny tried, but the grating was jammed.

We cast around for something to use as

a lever, but there did not seem to be a scrap of metal in the cellar. Edward said there had once been an ancient tool-box among the rubbish, but he couldn't remember what might be in it. The tool-box would be too heavy to float. Once again the men picked up their planks and probed the floor. Edward discovered the body of Crisp. That was a horrible moment. In silence he gathered up the body and carried it to the sideboard, which still stood in its original position. Everything else in the cellar, apart from the bunks, was moving by now.

They failed to find the tool-box on the floor. At last Edward thought to look inside the sideboard, and found it there. He set it high up on the steps and we all crowded round to inspect it. No chisels, no hammers . . . only a motley collection of nails, tacks, screws and a few large bolts, two of which measured the length of my hand. Nothing which would help us.

I sat on the top bunk, shivering, while the men wrenched at the grating with their bare hands. Finally they got it up. Johnny dived underneath to inspect the drain He came up with a double handful of tiny stones and mud.

'Cement mixture,' said Edward. 'Not properly set. They must have done the job in a hurry this afternoon. We can ladle it out, perhaps. We'll use the planks as scoops, contrive some boxes from other planks and ladle it into them, or else it will slide back as we clear the hole . . .'

I said, 'Edward, isn't there some rope down here? I don't like it when you disappear underwater. Suppose you don't come up? You could easily knock yourself out underwater, and I couldn't help.'

As if to support my proposal, when Johnny came up again, he put his hand to his head and brought it away with blood on his fingers. Neither man took any notice of my suggestion. I don't think they'd even heard me.

'The cement's inside a drum of some kind,' said Johnny. 'Metal. I can feel all round the rim. It's circular, and almost completely blocking the drain. There's not enough room for you to get your hands down between it and the sides of the manhole, but there's enough room for the water to come up. Clever, really.'

Edward went under to investigate, while Johnny wiped his forehead of blood, and panted. I took off my once-beautiful dress, laid it on the top bunk, and climbed down to search for some rope. The clinging dress would only hamper my movements and it would be no protection against the spars of wood and broken pieces of furniture which were bobbing around in the water.

'Dustbin!' gasped Edward, coming up for air. 'Old metal dustbin, let down into the drain and filled with stones and ready-mix cement. Luckily for us they've got the proportions wrong and it hasn't set yet.'

The men started to scoop out stones and cement. The water was up to my breastbone and icy. I wondered how the men were being affected by the cold, for although both were strong and well-built, neither had been through an easy time that day, neither had eaten that evening, and both had been drugged. Edward was bearing up well; it looked as if he might beat the drug, but he was slow and heavy in his movements. Johnny was fresher, even though he had played tennis that afternoon.

I couldn't find any rope. I tried the sideboard first, and then waded round the cellar, picking up planks and chairs and trying to jam them into the bottom bunk so that they would not impede the men in their work. I was almost round when I tripped and fell into the water, going right under. More shocked than hurt, I spluttered to the surface. I had fallen over something soft. Dragging it to the sideboard, I found I had tripped over a bolster full of old clothes. Useful, if they hadn't already been as saturated with water as the clothes we had on. Edward had discarded his jacket and was working in shirtsleeves; both men's clothes were already torn and muddied.

And still the waters rose.

'It's no good,' said Johnny, leaning on his plank. 'The further down we go, the harder it is to clear. The water will soon be too deep for us to work down there. Isn't there a pickaxe? Couldn't we break into the drain farther along and let the water out that way?'

'I can't be sure of the exact run of the drain,' said Edward, 'and anyway, we've already searched for tools. There aren't any. Let's take a breather and think again.'

As they waded to the bunks, I ducked under the water to inspect the manhole for myself. I'd always been a good swimmer, and it would be no hardship for me to stay underwater a while. In fact, it took only a moment to certify my guess.

As I came up for air, 'What are you doing, Kit?' Edward was angry with me. 'What a fright you gave me! I thought I told you to keep out of the way!'

'Darling, if you go on like that, I'll turn Women's Lib! I'm just as brave as you are, and I've got far more brains. Whoever it was put that dustbin down there had to knock the handles off first, in order to get it to fit within the diameter of the manhole . . . right? So he left four holes, two on either side of the dustbin, about a handsbreadth down, where the handles had been joined on . . . right? So why can't you thread something through the holes and lift the dustbin, complete with contents, clear of the drain?'

The men looked at each other, struggling with their worser selves. They didn't want to admit they'd overlooked the obvious, but both

147

saw I was right.

'Leverage,' said Johnny, squinting at the planks which floated around them. 'I could rig up a sheerlegs . . .'

'No rope,' said Edward. 'No chains. We'd be wasting our time. I think I ought to tackle the door. Maybe I can make some impression . . .'

'You know perfectly well you can't make an impression on an oak door with your bare hands,' I said. 'There are plenty of old clothes in that bolster. I'll make you all the ropes you need, if you do the engineering.'

For all my boasting, I was quite pleased to have the men take me by the arms and escort me to the steps. That water was getting too deep for me.

'Promise me you'll stay there?' said Edward. 'Be good, Kit, for my sake. I shan't have a moment's peace if I know you're in danger.'

'I'll turn over a new leaf.'

'Do we trust her?' Johnny enquired of his father.

'She means it when she looks you in the eye,' Edward explained. 'But watch out if she avoids looking at you.'

Johnny's laugh lightened the gloom, but the next half-hour was the stuff from which nightmares are born. I pierced holes in the seams of old clothes, using a file from the tool-box, rent the fabric into strips and plaited the strips into ropes. The men slipped and cursed and heaved wood around, with the water ever rising around them. They raised a tripod of timber over the manhole, and secured it with my makeshift ropes. By that time the debris I had piled into place on the lower bunk had floated free again, and the water was sucking at the corpse of Crisp on the sideboard.

Johnny slipped and fell. He was a long time coming up, and Edward dropped the planks he was carrying to dive underwater for his son. That was the worst moment of my life; I sat there with my hands clenched, trying not to scream. I prayed. I vowed to sacrifice something which was of importance to me, if only the men were spared. I would give up drink, and become a teetotaller, I would . . .

They surfaced. Johnny was half-conscious and waterlogged. Edward went into a life-saving act and deposited Johnny heavily on my lap before taking another supply of rope back to the tripod.

Johnny coughed and spluttered back to life in my arms. It was the first time I'd touched him since he was a few weeks old, and he was now twice my weight. I unwound the bandages from his wrists and bound the cut on his forehead, which was still bleeding.

'Better now!' he gasped. He tried to sit up. I pressed him back. 'My father!' he cried.

Edward was nowhere to be seen. For a moment we both feared he had drowned. Then Edward surfaced, whipped back his hair, and went under again.

'He's trying to wedge bolts from the tool-box across the holes left by the dustbin handles,' said Johnny. 'Then we can tie rope round the chisels, hoist it over the sheerlegs and pull the dustbin up out of the hole.' He made as if to jump back in, but I held him back, and he was so shaken that he didn't hold me off. Edward got one bolt fixed at the third try. The second took much longer, a further five nerve-racking minutes. The water was around his chest now, and it was easier to swim than wade.

'He's strong for his age,' commented Johnny.

'He's only forty-two, and you won't live as long as that if you don't take better care of yourself. I insist that you two rope yourselves together from now on.'

'You sound just like Mum; "Have you got your handkerchief? Don't forget your overcoat!"' He flicked my cheek. 'You're all right,' he said. He tied one end of a rope round his waist, coiled the rest round his shoulders, gave me an elaborate salute and plunged back into the water.

The next ten minutes were spent in hectic and fruitless efforts to raise the dustbin. I moved the tool-box and the remaining heap of cast-off clothes to the top step while the men struggled and spoke of counterpoises and weights. They lashed some planks together and fitted them over the tripod. One end of this makeshift crane now depended over the manhole, and Edward dived again and again to attach a rope from this to the bolts lodged in the dustbin's sides. Then the two men gathered all the driftwood they could find and lashed it to the free end of the balancing plank. It didn't shift the dustbin, although the ropes strained taut.

'I'll climb on it,' panted Johnny. 'We haven't anything else heavy enough to raise it. We couldn't shift the sideboard, and haven't enough ropes to spare to reach . . .'

'Will the ropes stand the strain?'

'Must do. We've only got to get it moving a few inches, put in a wedge, the force of the water will help us once we've made some headway . . . how deep does it usually run in the drain?'

'Before I diverted it? Knee-deep, I'd say.'

Johnny mounted on Edward's shoulders and climbed on the balancing plank. My ropes strained and stretched. Edward leaped at the plank and hung on to it, adding his weight to Johnny's. Was it my imagination, or were their bodies sinking towards the water?

SIX

'It's going down!' I shrieked. I stood up and yelled and waved my arms around, for the level of the water was now stationary, and now,very slowly, dropping. It crept down the brick wall beside me, leaving a deposit of wet sludge behind it. Suddenly debris was circling round, converging on Edward, who was gallantly holding on to Johnny and the plank. He was going to be battered by everything loose in the cellar, in its whirlpool withdrawal.

'Hang on another minute!' panted Johnny. 'It's coming up. The force of the stream below is helping to keep the bin up . . .'

The water made sucking noises as the battered drum rose slowly into sight. My ropes were stretched to their limit. One was uncurling . . . unfurling . . . going to give way . . .

I dived into the water and swam in a rapid crawl to the rescue. Something buffeted my shoulder, but I kept on. Just as the rope was about to part, I reached the bin and thrust at it, forcing it away from me, over on to its side. It tipped and fell, but now it was only halfway over the whole, and Edward could release his grip on Johnny to help me shove the bin out of the way. Johnny scrambled down to, help us.

Then the water was dragging at us, trying to suck us down into the drain with all the loose shale and cement and wine racks and broken furniture and planks that had been floating around. We fought our way back to the steps and huddled with our arms round each other, bruised, tired and chilled.

'What I'd give for a brandy,' groaned

Edward.

I recalled with annoyance that I was never going to drink brandy again. What a pity. I twisted wet strands of hair on to the top of my head.

'I must look awful,' I said. 'The very latest look for bathing; gilt sandals, nylon bra and pants, and a lot of jewellery! What a pity I've only got one ear-ring left!'

Edward started to say that he thought I looked marvellous, but Johnny laughed. Edward's lips relaxed and he admitted that yes, I wasn't looking quite my normal self. There was hope for my union with Edward if he could love me looking like a corpse out of a horror film.

'What now?' asked Johnny, surveying the cellar as the water level dropped lower. Everything movable was now jammed in a tight pack over the manhole, leaving only the bunk beds and the sideboard in their original positions.

We looked at our watches. Mine had stopped, Johnny's was smashed, but Edward's still worked. It was nearly midnight. We supposed the party was still carrying on way above us, although we could hear nothing of it.

'I'll start on the door when we've had a rest,' said Edward. 'Using a bolt as a hammer, I could maybe chip a hole through, using a bundle of nails tied together with wire as a chisel.'

I could see that Johnny thought as little of the plan as I did, but it was plain that doing something would be better than doing nothing, and equally plain that if we sat still for long we would slide into sleep and die. The cold in the cellar was intense. I curled up between the two men while they discussed what they ought to do if Lewis were foolish enough to check on us by opening the cellar door.

'Plenty of stuff to clobber him with here,' mused Johnny. 'Planks, an old sock filled with shale and cement mixture. I could stand flat against the wall at the head of the stairs and clobber him before he knows what's happening!'

We looked at the narrow landing at the head of the stairs and realised it wasn't going to be as easy as Johnny made out to catch Lewis. The door opened into the larder, so Lewis need only open it, standing well back, to see that the cellar was no longer flooded and that we were therefore alive. Indeed, if he had any sense, he would not touch the door to the cellar, for one look at the larder floor would show him that the water had failed to rise to the ceiling of the cellar. He would report to Amy that there was no tale-tell water on the larder floor, and . . .

'She will guess we are still alive and have found some way to divert the floods from inside. She will take no chances,' said Edward. 'Whether she needs proof of my death or not, she will not risk a murder charge. Better to leave us to starve and wait the seven years for presumption of my death. No, we've got to get out of here by ourselves, and the only way out is through that door.'

'New bolts top and bottom,' I muttered.

'It's oak,' said Johnny. 'It'll take for ever to get through that with what tools we have.'

'We have all the time in the world,' said Edward. 'No one will disturb us. I agree that it may take days for us to carve a way out, but that's better than dying, isn't it? We'll take it in turns. I'll start.'

I pointed to the floor. 'Look, the water is rising again!'

'The outlet's blocked with all that debris,' said Johnny, jumping down. 'We'll have to clear it again before we can start on the door.' We formed a human chain to clear the hole and drag the dustbin clear of the hole. The water sank rapidly once more, until it was running cleanly along the channel under our feet. Edward rescued the bolts, disentangled some wire from the bunk where it had been used to tie me up, and started chipping away at the door.

I crouched at the edge of the manhole, fascinated by the water as it slipped darkly away under my feet. Amy could not yet have diverted the water back through the sprinkler system or it would not be flowing so fast. Perhaps she descended to the larder every hour or so to check on the level of the water. How soon would she guess that something had gone wrong with her plan, and what action would she take then?

I shivered. I had a great respect for Amy.

'Look at this!' cried Johnny. He showed me a weird contraption taped to the bottom of the dustbin. He raised his voice to attract Edward's attention. 'Know anything about dynamite? There's some fixed here—they must have intended to set it off later on, in order to clear the channel for the water.'

'Don't touch it!' warned Edward.

It turned out that neither man knew anything about explosives.

'If it had a clock on it,' said Johnny, 'we could put it against the cellar door, wait for it to go off, and then walk out of here.'

'But it doesn't have a clock,' said Edward, 'which means that it is going to be detonated electrically at some time convenient to Amy. We daren't meddle with it ourselves. We can't use it. We mustn't try to alter its position or defuse it. We can't put the bin against the door and hope for the best because it might blow up while one of us is working there. Our best bet is to cart the bin into one corner of the cellar, build a barricade round it with whatever we can lay hands on, and pray!'

So that's what we did. I didn't like it. Johnny didn't like it. Nobody liked it. But it was the only thing we could do.

156

Edward went back to the door, and I returned to the manhole.

'Couldn't we float a message down the drain?' I asked.

'Don't think so,' said Edward. 'You'll find a grating down-stream. I put it there a while ago to catch any debris which might come down the drain.'

Johnny came to look. He got down into the manhole, and felt around. He said he thought he could probably get the grating out, if Edward thought it was worth the effort.

'It's almost wide enough for me to go down the drain myself,' said Johnny. 'How far is it from here to the lake?'

Edward dropped his makeshift tools in horror. 'Don't think of it! It must be fifty metres to the lake. Remember how the lawn slopes to the lake . . . the drain drops sharply down below the house and enters the lake about two metres down . . . it would not be possible for anyone to swim all that way underwater. Besides, the drain is too narrow for any man—for any-one to get through it. It may even get narrower farther down.'

Johnny was frowning. Edward had said first that 'no man' could get through the drain, and then had amended it to 'no one'. He was right in thinking that a man as broad in the shoulder as himself or Johnny would be stuck before he got far. But a woman—a small woman, used to swimming underwater—might get through if the tunnel did not narrow at the lake end.

Johnny looked at me. 'Fifty metres?' he queried, too softly for Edward to hear.

'I don't think it's fifty metres. Maybe forty.'

'Underwater, through a drain . . .' Reluctantly he shook his head. 'He's right. You mustn't risk it.'

'Get the grating out, anyway. We'll try to send a message down through the drain.'

'A paper boat? A message in a bottle? Why not?'

But I knew there were no bottles in the cellar, and a paper boat would be swamped and sink in that water-filled channel. Nevertheless, I rummaged around while Johnny replaced his tripod, mended the rope and set about pulling the grating out of the drain. I quartered the floor of the cellar for Edward's pen-knife, but there was no sign of it. I suppose it had been sucked down into the drain when the water receded. I shivered with fear because I knew that I was going to have to go down the drain. We could not afford to wait for Amy to discover that her scheme had failed. Already Edward's movements were dragging, and Johnny moved like a sleep-walker. The chill of the cellar would finish us all off, even if Amy decided to leave us to starve to death, and did not descend on us with Lewis and the chauffeur to beat our brains out and throw us into a trench dug by night in the woods . . .

'What are you doing?' asked Edward, as I climbed the stairs to rummage once more in the bolster.

I explained once more that I was looking for something to send through the drain to attract attention to our plight. There was nothing left in the tool-box to help us.

He caught at my arm. 'You mustn't go down there yourself. Promise? It's too dangerous. I couldn't bear it.'

'I'm a good swimmer.'

'Not that good. Not good enough for fifty metres underwater. Promise me? The lake is full of reeds, too. It's not safe to swim there, which is why I built the pool. Promise!'

He was right, of course. I promised.

'Thanks, Kit. You're such a headstrong little person that I was afraid you'd try it and drown. I know you'll keep a promise. You always mean what you say when you look me in the eye, don't you?'

'Got it!' cried Johnny. He had the grating half in and half out of the manhole. I scrambled down to help him, leaving Edward tapping away at the door. He had hardly made any impression on it. We could not get the grating out into the cellar, so eventually we pushed it back up the drain, against the flow of water, and wedged it there. The way was open to the lake, but I had promised not to take it.

And then we had our first real stroke of luck. Even as Johnny and I sat there above

159

the manhole, the flow of water slackened and sank to a trickle. We stared down, knowing that Amy must have turned the course of the stream back into the sprinkler system, which meant that very soon Lewis would come to see what had happened to us . . .

It also meant that there would not be fifty or forty, or even thirty metres of submerged drain between us and the lake. Maybe fifteen or twenty, depending on how far beneath the waters of the lake the drain came out.

I had to go, and go quickly before Edward realised what I intended to do. I would be breaking my promise to him, but since circumstances had changed since I had given it, I didn't worry too much about that. What I did worry about was Edward's reaction once he found I had gone.

I slipped through the manhole into the drain. Johnny helped me down. He was made of the same stuff as I was, and he wouldn't hinder me, even though he knew the risk I was running.

'Keep him sane for me!' I whispered. I crouched. I crawled rapidly down the drain Even as I went I heard Edward's voice echo down the tunnel behind me . . . 'Kit!'

It was slimy in the tunnel, and quite, quite horrible. I like water, and I like swimming, but I don't like underground places, and I don't like crawling through slime. Twice I stopped and fought panic, but I couldn't turn round and go back since the tunnel only just accepted me. It never occurred to me to go back up the drain the way I'd come. My chief fear was that Amy would discover that the water was not yet over the store-room floor, and would send the spring water through the drain again, which would drown me for sure.

I paddled on. When I looked back under my arm I could see a prick of light in the darkness where the manhole let light in from the cellar. Then the walls of the drain bent to the left and I lost even that cheering ray of light.

The slime became liquid, and I splashed on. I stopped when the filthy water lapped my elbows, fighting panic. I went over the arguments once more and came to the same conclusion. If I went on, I might drown but I had a fifty-fifty chance of fighting my way through into the lake, and once in the lake I could attract attention ... call for help ...

I went on. When the water reached my mouth, I took a deep breath and started to swim. In a couple of strokes I was underwater and brushing against the sides of the tunnel.

I don't ever want to do anything like that again. It was not nice, not at all.

I bumped my head, my shoulder and my thigh, and I was blind in that filthy dark water. Then I thought I was going to pass out, for there was a thudding in my head and my lungs were pressed so flat that . . . lights flashed across my retina and I resigned myself to death

. . . but it was the moon and the fairy lights shining through the depths of the lake that I saw. I came shooting up through the reeds, gasping, as fireworks burst into life, repeating their brilliance in the waters around me.

I was worn out. I struggled through the reeds, half threshing, half pulling myself to the bank.

'Paul!' A well-known voice spoke sharply above my head. 'Come here, quickly!'

A jewelled hand caught hold of mine, and hauled me on to the soft grass. Joan.

Surfacing near to Joan and Paul was the second piece of good luck we had that night, for of all the people I knew, they were the best equipped to comprehend the situation and act on it. At first Paul wanted to go direct to a phone and call the police, but when I threatened to have hysterics, he assured me he would do nothing to attract attention until we had rescued Edward and Johnny. My unconventional arrival on the bank of the lake had caused little or no commotion since the fireworks display was well under way and most people were watching that. Joan took off her brocade evening coat and made me put it on. Then, arm in arm, we strolled up the lawn to the house. Paul darted off to have a word with Jack Straker, asking him to drum up reinforcements, but rejoined us by the time we reached the patio. The band had stopped playing for the duration of the fireworks

162

display, and the floodlights had been turned out, so that we were able to pass through the crowd of guests without remark.

'Amy is down by the swimming pool,' said Paul. 'James is propping up the bar under the trees over there . . . don't look! Piers is in with a crowd of his friends down by the lake, but I don't know where old man Coulster is. Someone reported he'd been feeling ill and had gone to lie down. I can't see either Lewis or the chauffeur. Jack's going to see if he can locate them. Jack was worried about you; thought you'd eloped with Edward!'

'Not tonight, Josephine!' I said, and tried not to scream with hysterical laughter at my witticism.

'This way.' Paul directed us through the main reception rooms, filled with stands of flowers, and through a baize door into a dark corridor.

I stumbled. Joan's coat was too long for me, and I had fallen over its hem.

'Kit, can you manage? Darling, you're shaking! Wouldn't you like to sit down and rest while Paul gets the men out?'

I shook my head. 'If Edward is still alive, he's going to half kill me for going down that drain.'

'A larder, did you say?' Paul tried various doors. He located Amy's office, and I pointed to a corridor at right-angles to the one in which we stood.

A burly figure in evening dress pounded along the corridor behind us, and I put both hands over my mouth to stifle a scream. It was Fred, his genial face strained with anxiety.

'Hush!' said Paul, testing the larder door. It was locked.

Joan pulled me aside and put her arms round me while the two men set their shoulders to the door. At the third charge it gave, and they stumbled into the larder. The floor was quite dry. Lewis's waders stood in one corner.

'Men hate being rescued by women,' I said to Joan. 'And he'll be furious with me because I've given him such a bad scare.'

'If I were you, I'd faint!' advised Joan, with one of her wicked grins.

'I can't faint on demand!'

Paul unbolted the cellar door, and called out that we were friends. Two filthy, ragged men lurched into the larder, causing their friends to draw back. One of the wild men tore me from Joan, shook me, and said he was going to thrash the life out of me. The other propped himself against the wall and grinned at me. He said Edward had tried to go down the drain after me, and that there had been a slight—er—altercation about it. In other words, he'd had to fight Edward in order to stop him committing suicide.

'I'll half kill you, Kit!' said Edward, hugging me so fiercely that I cried out. His threats

164

gave me enormous pleasure, for I was sure he had never in his life before felt moved to lay a finger on a woman in that way.

I wound my arms round his neck and whispered that I'd been terribly afraid, and that I'd never do it again . . .

'Until the next time you think you know better than me!'

There was a cry from Joan. Johnny was half-lying on the floor, with Paul trying to lift him. Johnny's bandage had slipped. Blood was dribbling down the side of his face and his skin was waxen under the grime.

Edward put me down and assumed control of the situation. Joan and Fred were to take Johnny and me through into Edward's study, ring for the police and send someone to find a doctor. In the meantime, Paul could help Edward and Jack to search out the conspirators.

Voices were to be heard in the passageway. Jack's alarmed face appeared in the doorway. He had been keeping watch outside. Edward drew him into the larder and motioned him to stand opposite Fred, flanking the door to the corridor.

'. . . I told you not to be so hasty. If the water hasn't reached the larder floor, then it is simply not rising as fast as you calculated it would, and we will have to keep pumping it in until it is up to the required level.' It was the Alderman speaking. Someone else replied, but

I couldn't make out what he said.

'No, no,' said the Alderman testily. 'I'm feeling all right now. It was the excitement and having to deal with Edward by myself that made me feel unwell, but your taking so long to drive the Rolls round to the other side of the lake left me with no alternative. Well, what are you waiting for? Turn the water back into the cellar again. We'll give it another hour. There may be some outlet we don't know about from the cellar . . .'

'The larder door is open!' That was Lewis's voice. He appeared in the doorway. Jack and Fred pulled him into the larder, Edward hit him, and they all piled on top of their victim. Lewis squawked once, and then lay still.

'What . . .?' asked the Alderman, shuffling to the door. Behind him there loomed another man, in a chauffeur's uniform.

'Welcome!' said Edward.

All the forcefulness drained out of the Alderman. He leaned against the doorpost and closed his eyes. Edward grabbed the chauffeur's shoulder and drew him, unresisting, into the larder.

'Tie them up,' said Edward. 'Put them in the cellar and bolt the door.'

'No !' sighed the Alderman.

'No,' Edward agreed. 'Not you. I want a word with you. I want to know how many of you are involved.'

'Not Piers,' said the Alderman, faintly. 'I

know he's the only one you care about.'

Edward took his arm and beckoned the rest of us to follow him. Fred and Paul stayed behind to dispose of the minor villains. We processed through the house to Edward's study. Johnny had recovered sufficiently to walk, with his arm round my shoulders. Tinker appeared, running, and took Johnny off me, to lay him on a settee. Someone lit a fire in the grate, someone else pushed me down beside Johnny. Edward was explaining, everyone else was exclaiming. Someone dashed off for a doctor who happened to be among the guests. Con and Bet hurried in; Con hurried out with another man to collect the Rolls, which had all my clothes in it. Sheila arrived with some food, and Morton with some drinks. A doctor materialised, and said he'd better stitch the cut on Johnny's head before he was packed off to bed. I helped him. A large brandy appeared at my elbow; I nearly drank it, then remembered my vow and asked for hot sugared tea instead. A woollen robe appeared and was put around my shoulders, while another was draped over Johnny.

Silence.

Everyone turned to the doorway. Amy stood there, in her beautiful black velvet dress, with diamonds shimmering at her wrists and ears. The powder stood out on her face and her eyes were like points of steel. She saw us, realised her plan had miscarried, but refused to admit defeat.

She inspected her father, sagging in an armchair, and discounted him as an ally. She was on her own. She was magnificent.

'Has there been an accident?' she asked, arching painted eyebrows. 'Edward, you should not desert your guests like this! I have been looking for you everywhere. There is some absurd rumour going round to the effect that you've run off with the Neely woman . . . I suppose you fell into the lake together! You should have more sense at your age!'

The doctor went on stitching Johnny's cut, but everyone else stood still. Everyone but Edward. He had stripped off his shirt, and was donning a dressing-gown. He belted it, and then walked over to a desk and sat down.

'Just in time, Amy. We only need to collect your brother and Piers to have everyone accounted for by the time the police arrive.'

'The police?' She laughed. 'What on earth for?'

Such was the force of her personality that for a dizzy moment I wondered whether I had imagined the events of the evening.

'Lewis and your chauffeur are locked in the cellar,' said Edward. 'There are witnesses to your father's involvement. Your brother was undoubtedly in the plot, as was Piers. If you will allow me one moment in which to write out my resignation as managing director, I will phone the police to clear up the mess.'

'Stop!' said Amy. 'Why destroy yourself?'

Edward picked up a pen, took off the cap, and selected a sheet of paper. He began to write.

'There must be some way to make you see sense,' said Amy. 'Oh, I see what this is . . . an elaborate plot to make me agree to a divorce. Well, if it means that much to you, I will agree. I will not contest a divorce, and I will not ask for maintenance. Nor will I ask you to sell this house. Keep it. I suppose I was partly to blame, in telling Lewis how much I resented your leaving me. Poor Lewis! In the cellar? I can hardly believe that he has actually taken steps to . . . well, tell me! What is the lad supposed to have done?'

Edward went on writing.

Amy put a hand to her head and rubbed it. 'I am not well!' She was acting, we could all see that. 'I've been taking pills for some time— in secret. Tranquillisers.' She was improvising, but making a good job of her story. 'I have been under a great strain. Perhaps I have said and done things which I cannot now remember saying or doing. Perhaps I ought to go as a voluntary patient to the Greenham Clinic for a while Yes, that is what I will do. I shall have treatment there. Quietly, without scandal. There is no need to call the police.'

'And the rest of them? Do you intend to take them into the Clinic with you? Are they all supposed to have been suffering from nervous breakdowns?'

'No, of course not. My father is an old man and ill.' This was self-evident. 'He will resign from the Council. He will resign from his position as Chairman at the Mills. He will go abroad for his health. The Seychelles, perhaps.'

'Leaving the Mills without anyone to operate them?'

'You will reconsider your decision to resign, I'm sure. As for my brother, he knew little of this. He agreed to bring Mrs Neely here in order to kill scandal, but that is all. He is too frivolous a creature to be depended on in a crisis.'

'You can't talk Piers out of it so easily. He wasn't here when Mrs Neely rang last night, and therefore must have been with you, and in the plot.'

'Not so. He acted as chauffeur for me, since it was Green's night off. He drove me to Father's house first, and then I sent him to fetch James, which he did. When James arrived I sent Piers home. The boy is too highly-strung for this work.'

Edward was pleased about that. But he went on writing.

'As for Lewis and the chauffeur,' said Amy, 'they obeyed my orders, that's all. Orders which I must have given when I was not myself. Lewis is a poor, weak fool who thought to step into your shoes. Of course

170

there was no question of marrying him. I used him, merely. The chauffeur knows little, except that I wanted the Rolls driven round the lake, and some work done in the cellar to stop a leak in the drain. He is a pawn. I suggest you take statements from them and let them go. You could tell them to be out of town by tomorrow night or you will give the statements to the police. They will disappear and you will never hear of them again. Lewis will lose his thriving business, which would be sufficient punishment, don't you think?'

'I'm not in the business of apportioning blame or punishment. I'm resigning, and then ringing the police.' Edward read through what he had written, signed it, folded it up and handed it to Amy. He reached for the phone.

'Wait!' Amy's composure was beginning to break up. She fiddled with the letter of resignation, then crumpled it up and threw it into the fireplace. She turned to Johnny, who was conscious but blurry-eyed. The doctor had finished stitching the cut, and was now getting out some pills.

'You—John Blake, or whatever your name is! I've heard you want to go into the Mills one day. You've even been round them with Edward . . . with your father, haven't you? Well, how about our appointing you as a director? We could give you some shares, and you could walk into the place tomorrow on equal terms with Piers . . . with your half-brother.'

'Is she for real?' Johnny asked me. 'If my father doesn't think I should work for him till I'm qualified, then what good would I be to him as a director?' He turned to Amy, trying to be courteous to someone who was obviously in need of medical attention. 'I'm not trained yet,' he said. 'I've only just left school.'

Edward grinned. Johnny's reply had given him enormous pleasure. Amy flushed, and then turned to me.

'My father will sell you his shares, voting stock and all. We could have an Extraordinary General Meeting and vote you on to the Board. You could have enough shares to give Edward a controlling interest in the Mills.'

For a moment I was tempted, but not enough.

'It would also give me a hold on Edward, wouldn't it? Well, I don't want him under that sort of obligation to me. Besides,' I lied, speaking to the ceiling above her head, 'My late husband tied up all my money in a trust fund, and Edward won't be able to touch it when he marries me!'

Edward laughed. 'Sorry, Amy. You haven't a single thing to offer that we want. I don't want this house, not any more. You know very well that it was a bribe, offered me in compensation for what I couldn't have. Now that Kit is free, I'll gladly give up White Wings. In fact, I want to do so. I want to start fresh.

172

You have had my letter of resignation. There are plenty of people here to witness what you've done with it. Very well. I will call an Extraordinary General Meeting tomorrow and those of you who are out on bail can meet and receive my resignation in person. I shall take my money out of the Mills and go elsewhere.'

'You're paying a high price for her,' said Amy.

'I don't think so,' said Edward, the accountant. He pulled the phone towards him, dialled and asked for the police.

'Fools!' Amy threw her words at us like knives, and like knives they wounded. 'You, Edward; you'll regret having thrown away everything you've worked for. You won't be able to satisfy her, either. Remember how many men she went with before you? How long will it be before she leaves you for someone else? You, boy! In the years to come you'll cry your eyes out thinking of the opportunity you threw away. And you, Kit Jeffries! Remember my words if and when you ever get him into bed with you. You've got yourself a poor bargain!'

'Not so!' I said, drawing myself up to my full height. 'You seem to forget that Edward has two fine sons already, and that we are still young enough to have more. Personally,' I drawled, 'I have always found Edward extremely responsive.'

Someone laughed. Amy tried to speak, and

failed. I had dealt her a blow from which she would not recover.

Jack held the door open for her. 'The Queen is dead. Long live the Queen!' he said. 'Amy, why don't you take your father away and get him to lie down until the police come? He looks all in to me.'

The Alderman staggered to his feet and made it to the door. Amy's eyes cleared a path for her through our friends. She left, but her parting words stayed in our minds.

*   *   *

Jack had not been motivated by anything but simple kindness when he suggested that Amy left the room, but she must have seen his words as an incentive to escape. She hurried through the house with her father, collected her car from the garage and drove off. Perhaps she hoped to get herself to the Clinic and cheat the police of their quarry; perhaps she simply lost her nerve for once, and abandoned herself to the instinct to run away. Next morning her car was found upside down in a field below a sharp bend in the road, no more than a mile from White Wings. The Alderman was dead, and Amy badly injured. She died the following night without having regained consciousness.

Since it was proved at the inquest that the Alderman had died of natural causes—another heart attack—before the crash, it was assumed

174

that in his final agony he had clutched either at Amy or the steering wheel, thus causing the car to go off the road. A verdict of Accidental Death was therefore recorded for Amy.

The irony of it was that since the Alderman had died before his daughter, and she was his sole legatee, all his money and his shares in the Mills passed to her; and since the Will Amy had signed on the day of her marriage had never been altered, everything which she possessed at the moment of her death passed to Edward. Thus at one stroke Edward inherited control of the Mills and most of the Coulster fortune. He was persuaded to withdraw his resignation—indeed, once Johnny and I had told him that we thought he ought to carry on, he didn't take much persuading.

I went to stay first with Paul and Joan, and then with Con and Bet. I would have preferred to be on my own, but there seemed to be some sort of conspiracy to see that I was never left alone. As a matter of fact, I did feel very tired for a long time after our adventure in the cellar, and I was grateful at first for their care of me. Later, I rebelled, and when no one would hear of my taking a house or a flat for myself, I volunteered to caretake for Fred while he took Sheila and the children away on an extended holiday.

Edward cleared up the mess left by Amy with his usual efficiency, but he became very grim and difficult to approach. His chief problem was what to do with Piers, who took the events of his birthday evening hard. There was little doubt that he had suspected something of the plot against us, and had deliberately closed his eyes to the knowledge. His guilt, remorse, and fear that he had lost his father's love drove him almost to the verge of breakdown. He was useless at the Mills, rude to his father, swore at me, and in short didn't know where or what he was. In the end James Coulster made the surprisingly sensible suggestion that Piers be packed off to university in order, or so he said, that Piers did not let Johnny get ahead of him in the world. I think perhaps Piers decided to go in order to give himself a breathing space, but whatever the reason, the decision was justified by events. Once away from the Coulster influence, and forced to rely on his own quite considerable talents, Piers began to grow up. The last time he was home I found myself scolding him exactly as I scold Johnny and, instead of swearing at me, he merely grinned. I am beginning to like the lad, and I think he is beginning to tolerate me at last.

Johnny managed to heal the breach between me and my sister Mary, for which I was very thankful. I humbly accept her frequent criticism of my extravagance and behaviour in exchange for becoming a sleeping partner in Tom's building firm.

The cut on Johnny's head healed well, and although he will have to face a variety of problems in the future ranging from the Blakes' wish for him to marry Sally, through a change of surname, to Piers' hostility when both boys finally enter the Mills together, I have no doubt that Johnny will continue to land on his feet.

Jack won his brown-haired Hazel, and I am godmother to their first child, a boy. Tinker has recently supplied me with a new car, and his son Dick has promised to take Johnny and Piers on a guided tour of the latest hot-spots when they are next home together.

By Christmas I was at my wits' end about Edward. He would not climb into bed with me because he said he wanted to prove his feeling for me was not just sex, but neither would he set a date for our wedding. The truth was, of course, he was afraid he would fail.

Finally I wrote him a note saying I was sorry that things hadn't worked out, that it would be best if I went back to America where, although I would be unhappy for a while, I would no doubt find someone to marry me. I delivered the note in person to his secretary at the Mills, and went home to make my preparations.

Within half an hour he arrived, in a very bad temper.

I was alone, of course. I was wearing a very becoming negligee, bought specially for the occasion. I protested, but not too much.

He put me over his knee. It hurt. I yelled, but not too loudly.

After that he demonstrated to our mutual satisfaction that I had been right about him, and Amy wrong. We were married the following week by special licence, and nine months later our darling daughter Carla was born.

We don't live at White Wings, but at Gresham Place, which is high on a hill outside the city, and has its own farm attached. We bought it with my money, and it is my responsibility to restore the decrepit house and non-productive farm. At the last count I was responsible for forty-one persons; for my husband and my daughter, for Johnny and Piers, who frequently stay with us at weekends, for the *au pair* girl and the resident nanny, for the gardener and his wife, who helps me in the house, and their son, who is on the wild side; also for the farmer and his wife and their three children, two dogs, three cats, four pet rabbits and eighteen pet mice. And if you don't consider pet mice are 'persons', I refer you to all the children on the place, who believe otherwise.

Oh, yes, I forgot to include one of the boys from Edward's club, who seems to find his way here most weekends and sometimes plays truant to help me with the hens. Are hens persons, too? Oh, I give up!

It was Edward's idea to give me all this

responsibility. He says the only way to keep me out of mischief is to keep me busy. My latest task has been to organise a gigantic christening party for Carla. I have a beautiful new dress from Dior for the occasion and only one big Problem.

How can I toast my daughter's health in water?